Through the Fire: A Woman's Journey

Karen —

Thank you for your support!

Yasmeen

4/30/21

Through the Fire: A Woman's Journey

Copyright © 2019 Yasmeen Abdur-Rahman

ISBN: 9781076239778

No part of this book may be reproduced or transmitted in any form or by any means, graphic, electronic, or mechanical, including photocopying, recording, taping, or by any information storage or retrieval system, without the permission in writing from the publisher.

Published by: Kindle Direct Publishing

Printed in the United States of America

This is a non-fiction book. All names depicted in this book were changed to protect the privacy of those who lived through my life experiences.

Book cover designer: Angie Alaya of Pro_ebook Covers

Professional photos taken by: Olga Fortunatova of Kazka Photography LLC

Praises for Yasmeen Abdur-Rahman's Book:

"Through the Fire: A Woman's Journey"

Love it already! You left me wanting more. I can't wait to read the book! It's not easy to be so open and so vulnerable! I applaud your courage! Coming from a family plagued with depression, your words hit home. Thank you for sharing your story! You're an inspiration! I wish you many blessings! (Betsy Perez, Newark, New Jersey)

WOW! This is so powerful Yasmeen! Despite your setbacks, I'm so proud of what you're accomplishing. You're a woman to be reckoned with and I am blessed to have you in my life! (Lise Richards, Atlanta, GA)

I'm not an African-American, but I can relate to everything you're saying Yasmeen. My family never said, "I love you" and still doesn't today. I know my mom cares about me, but to her it's a sign of weakness to say it or show it. I've also struggled with depression and self-confidence due to the lack of family support. I love your advice and would like to read the book. I think it will touch many women, especially in the American culture who are struggling to have it all or do it all. Sometimes we need to embrace who we are and enjoy who we are. (Laura, USA)

I'm an African-American and I'm married. I've been getting your emails for over a year or so now. I admire you. Most African-American women wouldn't give out advice and knowledge that you give free to your clients. I can tell that you're a good-hearted person. I pray that GOD blesses you and your son. Reading what I've read so far, the two chapters of your book is interesting enough that I would want to purchase it! I, myself, went through depression about six years ago and said that I would never see a 'shrink' or go on medications. Guess what, it happened, and I'm glad that I have family that loved me enough to find me help. GOD, bless you with your first book! (Rhonda Barron-Williams, USA)

I'm so glad your book is coming along so great! I read the whole thing and it is DEEP! In the part where you say you make jokes and put up a front, I hope you don't do that anymore. I want you to be happy and not acting. The things you wrote about I can relate to, because I was depressed and I didn't even know the reason why. I think you are such a great person. You have such a wonderful aura that attracts people to you. You're going to do great things! (Jasmine Sanchez, Belleville, NJ)

Yasmeen, this is good! All of what you say in these chapters that I have read is so true. I wish you much success in the writing of your book. I am sure that it will help many women. (Sharyn Bradby, Morristown, NJ)

Yasmeen, I want to thank you for sharing a part of your book and a part of yourself! Even though I am not African-American, I can fully understand what you are describing since I've gone through similar situations myself. I wish you the best with your book and all you do in your life – again, thank you for sharing. (Karen Faheemud-Deen, USA)

This was great! I totally agree with every word. I would never have thought that someone who shows such strength could have ever felt weak and tired. My brother is currently going through what you describe in your book. It helped me understand him better. For that, I thank you! Now I think you should send this to Oprah. She talks about books and such that aren't as good as this one. (Josephine Labriola, NJ)

Table of Contents

Praises for Yasmeen Abdur-Rahman's Book

Dedication

Foreword

Chapter 1: Welcome to the World, Baby Girl

Chapter 2: Growing Up, Jersey Style

Chapter 3: The Projects

Chapter 4: Blood Is Thicker Than Water . . . Or is it?

Chapter 5: Money Never Equals Happiness

Chapter 6: Sisterhood

Chapter 7: School Days

Chapter 8: What About Your Friends?

Chapter 9: Love, Lust and Lies

Chapter 10: Love is Blind: Get Your Third Eye Examined

Chapter 11: Until Death or the Other Woman Do Us Part

Chapter 12: A Fatherless Child

Chapter 13: Owning Your Own

Chapter 14: My View on Islam

Chapter 15: Black is Beautiful

Chapter 16: Coming Out of the Dark

Chapter 17: Dear Mama

Chapter 18: Through the Fire: A Woman's Journey

Acknowledgements

Dedication

My mother is the ultimate dedication to my life. There is a quote from the Quran that says: "Be grateful to me and to both your parents." Here GOD almighty, immediately after referring to His own right, speaks about the rights of the parents. A man came to the Seal of the Prophets and said: "Oh Prophet of GOD! Guide me, to whom should I be good in order to benefit completely from my good deed?" He said: "Be good to your mother." He said again: "And next to her?" The Prophet answered: "To your mother." The man said: "To what other person should be good?" The Prophet said: "To your father." To the one person on the earth who paid attention to my heart and understood me. Mother loved me unconditionally. She wished the best for me my entire life. She's on my mind every single day and still her memories bring me to tears.

Preface

My book is for all the women of the world who are divorced, single parents, struggling to raise their children on their own; married and unhappy; to all the women battling depression, low self-esteem and suffering from anxiety. To the women blinded by men who are not capable of honesty and commitment, and most importantly, any and every woman who can relate, grow and prosper from my life's story. For Muslim women wearing hijab every day representing Islam, this book is for you!

My request is that you refrain from passing judgment on my previous circumstances and choices, but rather appreciate my honesty. See me for the person I have become today!

Do you believe that GOD has a plan etched out for you and your life? When you empower yourself with faith in Allah (GOD), your light starts to shine beyond your wildest dreams.

Credentials

Yasmeen Abdur-Rahman was born in Orange, New Jersey. Although as an adult, she lived most of time in Union. Today, she resides in Cary, North Carolina. She's married and has one son. Yasmeen is an Author, Résumé Writer, and Life Coach. She's the owner of The Brownstone Workshop; a virtual business which was started in 1993. She graduated from Drake College of Business in New Jersey with a Business Diploma and from Malcolm X Shabazz High School. She received several awards, including "The Berkeley Schools Annual Awards for Outstanding Achievement in High School Business Education," and "The United States Achievement Academy – National Commemorative Certificate for the National Award Winner." She attended Union County College in Cranford, New Jersey majoring in Business Administration; took numerous business-related courses. She's a member of CoachVille.com, International Association of Coaches (IAC) and Home-Based Working Moms Organization (HBWM). Certified as a Minority Owned Business Enterprise with the Dept. of Administration Office for Historically Underutilized Businesses in North Carolina. A Contributing Columnist who wrote and published business-related articles for several online business newsletters, blogs and websites. Listed in the "Empire Who's Who – Empowering Executives & Professionals" registry that is viewed nationwide.

Foreword: Introduction to My Life

It's been my desire to write a book. Not just any book – I wanted to write my memoirs! Seeing my words, written across a massive piece of blank paper, is electrifying. My uncle once asked, "What have you done that people would want to read about it?" At first, his statement offended me, but then I began to recognize that our philosophies and life journeys are diverse from one another. Instead of responding out of resentment, my reply was, "You don't have to be 'famous' to write a book."

Finally, it feels gratifying to be able to talk about my personal and professional misfortunes without restrictions; my struggles as a single parent after divorce, marriage, entrepreneurship, being an African-American, and Muslim woman who weathered the storm after 9/11. It's my desire that in reading about my life experiences (especially the women who have made the same mistakes or went through the same issues) will grasp whatever challenges come our way. You should never give up hope!

In the end, telling the 'truth' is vital for our communities to grow and prosper, especially within the African-American communities. In my opinion, we need help. If you don't tell the truth, we're doomed to repeat too many bad behaviors. Let go of the slave mentality!

I pray that all who read my book feel the empathy, truthfulness, and impact of the valuable lessons that I have suffered. My experiences carved me into the woman that I am at the moment. I believe that everyone has a path and life purpose that Allah has decreed for them. It's up to us to live the experiences, bask in the abundance of His blessings, and hope that it brings us towards good in this world.

There are endless goals for me to achieve. Reaching these goals has placed an extraordinary desire in me to strive and soar far beyond my expectations of myself, and towards what some people say cannot be achieved. With this book, my memoirs, at last I can say that one of my wildest dreams has come true: I'm a published author and this is my testimony.

"Never forget the little things your parents told you when you were younger. Those same lessons, one way or another, come into full circle – in your relationships and throughout your life until the end of your life."

(Yasmeen Abdur-Rahman)

Chapter 1: Welcome to the World, Baby Girl

Most people who knew my parents say that they were stunned by my arrival. My mother was shocked to discover that another baby girl was on the way. When Mother found out that she was pregnant with me, my sister was in elementary school. Who thought that my parents would practically wait ten years to have another baby? While pregnant, she envisioned herself raising a boy. Mother knew that raising another daughter would require extra time that she didn't have to spare. With a son, Mother knew that Daddy would guide him towards manhood. Plus, there's a significant number of male mentors all over our family tree to mimic. However, on May 4, 1966, another baby girl showed up and that baby girl was ME!

According to Mother, I entered the world with a beautiful full head of long, black, curly hair – bright eyed and ready to take on the world. When it was time to give me a name, my parents bestowed the honor to my grandmother. Grandma or "Ma" as we called her, named me "Wendy." Ma was a quiet, mild-mannered woman. She didn't say much, but she was outspoken in her own way. She loved everyone. I recall her as a positive person who wished the best for others. She said this name came to her because it was windy on the day of my birth. While growing up, people used to wonder, "Where did your name come from?" Most of my peers were African-American and back in the sixties and seventies, this name was one and the same to little Caucasian girls. There was a restaurant called Wendy's but no other Wendy that we could associate with in my neighborhood. Today, while working or at a function and someone calls out "Wendy" I tend to pause in my spirit.

My parents have been married for so many years. They can't tell you how long without checking the date on their marriage license. By the way, where is the marriage license?

My memories of living with both parents are sketchy. When my parents' marriage began to collapse, I was too young to understand. I don't have any memories of us living together as a family. It makes me upset thinking about it. It's weird because without family exposure, we've been closer than ever. As time passed by, I didn't understand why my parents separated without getting a divorce. Both my parents said since they were not going to remarry, why go through the process? To this day, they remain legally married as husband and wife. I think Mother believed that Daddy would come back to Jersey and sweep her off her feet again. It never happened. Both are stubborn, but in every other way, they are opposite. It's hard to distinguish which characteristics or connections brought them together in the first place. At the beginning, love keeps you together, but most couples fall out of love quickly.

As most children with separated parents, I wondered how life would be if my parents were living as husband and wife. In my mind, Mother struggled while Daddy lived his life in another state. My parents were so different. I am sure it would have been rewarding to learn and grow from both of their experiences. Nevertheless, my chances to find out never happened. Did their separation rob me of my parental lifestyle with my parents? If Daddy maintained his presence in our family, my sister and I would've had a broader perspective on men, in general, especially in marriage. To date, my sister hasn't been married.

It's not too late to find answers to my questions. I wonder if Daddy's answers are different now that I'm an adult rather than his little girl. Guess I'll always be his little girl? Since he's such a serious-minded and no-nonsense person, having those conversations is intimidating. He speaks his mind even if you don't understand his logic. He tends to never think that your story is real based on what he believes or thinks should've happened. When you speak with him, you automatically go into defense mode because of his forced dialogue. It's evident that my defensive mode is from Daddy. He questions what's being told to him. It's like what you're saying isn't true because he didn't say it.

In my younger years, my allegiance to my Dad was strong. Most girls are closer to their mothers, but my case was different. I missed Daddy and thought about him relentlessly. Because of his absence, I became envious when speaking with friends who had both parents physically at home. It felt as if a part of my life were missing, or there should be an alternate ending. Everyone in our family says that we are as similar as twins are, and I totally agree. We look so much alike that you wouldn't need a DNA test to confirm it at all. We laugh and sound exactly the same. One day we were on the phone chatting. He said something funny. It was like hearing an echo over the phone. Daddy loves that I won't hesitate or bite my words when my point needs to get across to others, but that same feeling bothers him when we speak. I stand up for what I believe in and do not waiver for anyone. I "penny-pinch," (another characteristic of Daddy), but it helped me save up and purchase two brand new cars. It enabled me to live in my own place without going back home with Mother. After business school, my corporate employment finances allowed me to support family members and relocate to another state twice. Therefore, when people say to me "You're just like your father," in many ways, it's a compliment. It wouldn't surprise me if Daddy sleeps with a ton of money underneath his mattress. He's been jokingly described as a 'Black Jew.'

Daddy relocated to Hartford, Connecticut after he and Mother separated and although he kept in contact with us, my fondest memories are spending my summer vacations with him. He drove to New Jersey to pick me up for every summer. For two months out of every year, Daddy drove me out of the hood. Daddy's girlfriend, Edith, is so much like my mother. She treated me like one of her biological children. Her children loved me from day one and even called me their sister. It's obvious why Daddy was attracted to her beauty and qualities. She was compassionate, classy and hygienic. Her physical appearance placed toe-to-toe of a 30-year-old woman. She knew what to say if you were experiencing a problem and tried to help everyone. Edith and Mother talked on the phone each summer during my visits to Connecticut. Edith had full permission to act as one of my guardians – meaning, keep me in place. Every summer was a fun adventure! We took long drives through Connecticut, went to cook-outs, amusement parks, movies and spent quality time as a family. When school returned in the Fall, my summer vacation stories were different than most of my classmates back in Jersey.

Most kids in my school rarely traveled outside of Jersey. Most of my school-mates' parents never got married or even remained friends. My summer vacation stories were full of fun and fabulousness.

LIFE LESSONS:

Although my parents were married when their children were born, they're not together today. To have longevity in your marriage, you must work hard and value your marriage vows, but more importantly obey your Lord. It appears that Mother fell out of love. From Daddy's recollections, he fought to keep us together. He didn't want to leave us. He worked two full-time jobs. He took care of us but Mother wanted out of the marriage. Mother asked Daddy to leave. There is a saying that opposites attract, but not in this case.

Through my parent's marital process, it's obvious most women stay married to appease her parents and children. When she realized that the man she married wasn't necessarily the right man for her or perhaps she wasn't the right woman for him, they separated. In my opinion, it's like putting a bandage on a wound that needs immediate surgery. They grew up in an era where you just don't divorce. Once the respect is gone, the marriage is relatively over. Mother's comfort zone was about being financially taken care of by Daddy. At that time of her life and upbringing, that's what the women were taught. Mother was a housewife. Her job was to raise the children. Daddy worked and maintained the family.

It's no secret of the dating patterns of both my parents. Both were heavy in the dating game but never thought about coming back to their marriage.

Mom struggled with her monthly income because it didn't exceed those who retired from a traditional 9 to 5 job. As her daughter, my responsibility was to make sure she was happy. I respected and loved her for being my mother. She sacrificed and struggled while unexpectedly becoming a single parent. If it was possible for me to give her what she needed, that's what I did. In my opinion, when children become adults, they should take care of their parents. It's good-natured to be 'taken care of' but in the end, you're all you have and nothing is guaranteed in this life. These days, Daddy has several huge checks deposited in his account each month. He worked up until retirement age. Whenever Mother called him for support, he helped. They were legally married and he was responsible for his wife, regardless of where he resided or if the children of the marriage were grown. The responsibilities are dropped when you're divorced. As Muslims, most women become housewives and remained home with the younger children. This is the structure Daddy wanted from their marriage.

In the end, Mother gained my respect for taking control of her life and raising her children to be mature, independent, and respectful women. Money didn't deter her from her duties as our mother. She never stopped to have a pity party about what did or didn't happen for us. She took the bull by the horn and pushed forward. Those are the characteristics that are woven deep in my body from Mother. She was a fighter! Regardless of how and why things happened the way they did, she accomplished her job as a parent.

During a conversation once, Daddy expressed the demise of their marriage was due to Mother hanging out at bars with her oldest brother. Our family followed religious guidelines of Islam. Hanging out at bars, drinking, smoking and mixing with other men was out of the question.

In the end, growing up in the absence of Daddy broke my heart. Living with regrets isn't healthy. We had a long conversation about their marriage and separation. As the baby daughter, I felt most of their history was kept away from me. When we end our phone conversations, we say we love each other. Daddy recently relocated back to Alabama. As he became older, he stated that he wanted to be buried in Alabama with his parents and family. Today, he's content and happy.

"People tend to think that there's no better place than where they live right now. Move outside of your area. Just because you were born and raised there, doesn't mean that you can't find peace somewhere else."

(Yasmeen Abdur-Rahman)

Chapter 2: Growing Up, Jersey Style

After my parents separated, we moved to a 3-family house located at 357 Morris Avenue in Newark, NJ. We resided on the first floor. The toilet and the bathtub were in separate rooms. This was the first time in my life seeing a setup like this in an apartment. The brick front house was old but it stood out on our block. It was a cozy apartment.

My grandfather gave me a jet Black, German Shepherd named Smokey. Smokey was my first pet. He was the most irresistible dog that I have ever seen. He meant the world to me. Smokey was a part of the family for years but unfortunately, he was stolen from my backyard. This pointless act devastated me. Who would be so cruel to steal a little girl's dog? After Smokey disappeared, it traumatized me so much. I never thought about having another dog as a pet. Mother purchased two dozen gold fish and a medium-sized fish tank in an attempt to replace my feelings for Smokey.

Morris Avenue was a clean, quiet block in Newark. It was a peaceful, safe area in the early to late eighties. What I remember most is watching Mother depart extremely early in the mornings to go to work. She held down many jobs at once. She worked as a Bartender at Polly's Bar (my cousin's bar at the corner of our block) at night and during the day, cleaned houses in the affluent areas of Short Hills and West Orange. My whole life, she told me that she didn't take Daddy to court for child support. After Mother's death, Daddy's memory of their past was different. Mother trusted Daddy would take care of us even if he lived in another state. Mother told Daddy that we needed new coats and shoes every winter. If our shoes did not have holes at the bottom of them, he said 'there is no need for a new pair.' Mother never showed her frustrations with Daddy or said anything derogatory about his character to us. She carried the heavy burden of raising her daughters alone. Like most single parents, she found the strength to go on through the power of other strong women. She consistently went the extra mile to make us happy. Although we were not wealthy, we did not want for much. There was love in our home and despite the lack of material things (like a fancy car or a big screen television) we were happy. To us, we were happy and healthy because our refrigerator was full of food, there was heat, and the lights were on.

My grandfather, also known to the family as "Pop," lived on the third floor of the house on Morris Avenue. His apartment displayed unique, antique fixtures. Walking into Pop's apartment reminded me of a museum. Every room was full of objects without a theme but no one ever touched his stuff. Pop knew what every item represented and if anything was moved, he would know about it. Pop meant what he said and said what he meant. Some people thought he was a cruel and uncaring man, but he took care of his business. Pop never asked anyone for anything. He was a strong-willed, straightforward man but unfortunately, he was a heavy drinker. He often had a drink early in the mornings. As I look back, I believe it's safe to say he was an alcoholic. After getting drunk, he slept with his front door wide open. Thank GOD, back then crime wasn't as wicked as it is now because he could have been robbed or killed in his apartment. While sober, he loved to play cards. Playing cards were his main source of entertainment. Family members showed up on Friday nights with a deck of cards, ready to whip somebody's butt.

Ma was the total opposite of Pop. She was quiet and lovable while everyone got along with her. She didn't curse, drink, gamble or hang out at bars. I recall one incident when a male friend dropped Ma off at Pop's house. While Pop was sitting outside on the porch, he witnessed it with his own two eyes. Pop ran outside with a loaded gun and began to shoot at the man. Thank God, he missed because if not, Pop would have gone to jail. Later, in the years, Ma and Pop separated. Through all of the dysfunction, they both made a mark on our family structure.

When you see your grandparents, it's like looking at hundreds of people who came from the same bloodline. Today, all my grandparents are deceased. It would be gratifying to pick up the phone to call them for advice or to hear them critique something that happened in our families. They were all full of wisdom which can't be gathered through reading books. My love for them is still in my heart as they played a huge role in my life growing up as a teenager.

Pop never called me Wendy, but the nickname "Winchy," said it all! It seems like everyone I knew growing up had a nickname. Pop and I shared a special bond. We shared the same birthday: May 4th. For every birthday that we spent together, I baked a cake and carried it upstairs for our celebration. Some of his other grandchildren (my cousins) were jealous of our relationship. I remember how Pop would argue with Mom not to beat me or yell at me. He saved me from a butt whipping several times.

Pop purchased my first bike. I rode up and down the block every day. We lived on a one-way street and the traffic pattern of cars was light. He sat on the porch and watched me while I rode my bike. I can still see him in my mind. Sitting in the same spot on the porch, swinging his legs from side to side and smoking a cigar. I loved Pop so much. For a long time after his death, most of my free time was filled with tears. His love took up a huge space in my heart. In addition to Daddy, Pop was the leading man in my life. Today, I wished that my son could have met Pop. Both of my grandfathers were among the last of the "good ones."

My Aunt Rose and her husband, both deceased, lived on the second floor. Aunt Rose painted her entire apartment red and black. Back then, it was rare to see a bathroom painted all black or all red. She decorated her apartment as if she was a famous interior designer. She kept everything clean and tidy. My auntie said things without thinking but she was funny and didn't care what you thought either way. Growing up, Aunt Rose inspired me. She had a swag about herself that was contagious and I wanted to be just like her.

LIFE LESSONS:

Don't be afraid to live outside of where you were born and raised. Don't be afraid to venture out of your state or country. I have learned that people, places and things are different in good ways and bad ways. For me, leaving Jersey allowed me to compare where I was to where I am now. It has affected me on a personal, business and family level. Seeing outside of your front door, gives you the mindset not only to think outside of the box, but to see how others live their best lives. The sight of green grass on the ground and trees as tall as the hills are views of inspiration. It creates positivity to my spirit and the community. Not putting a wheel lock on my car took a little time to adjust to after relocating to North Carolina. A thought came to my mind when a co-worker and I went to the mall for lunch. She said, "Yasmeen, we don't use steering wheel locks in North Carolina." I was so embarrassed.

I was a little annoyed when Daddy asked me why I moved to North Carolina. Why set my limitations to only living in Jersey? He moved from Alabama to Jersey and from Jersey to Connecticut. My reaction was simple. While living in Jersey, my family rarely called or visited me. What did I have to stay for? In addition to that, the low crime rate was another motivating factor. Although gangs and crime are everywhere, it wasn't running rampant in North Carolina. Now I understand 'southern hospitality.'

"People tend to look down to people that live in the projects. They are human beings and no less of a human being than you are. Be careful who you toot your nose up to because Allah can make an example out of you."

(Yasmeen Abdur-Rahman)

Chapter 3: The Projects

It was great living in a house with all my extended family. People were around and you felt loved and protected. Things went on that way for years, until the Clinton Milk Company (which was located next door to us), purchased our house and all the land from the entire block. As a result, my family moved to the nearby projects called 'Hayes Home.'

We resided in an 8th floor apartment. The dark, smelly hallways were disgusting. When the elevators were not operational, which was quite often, we marched up eight flights of stairs. Sometimes we were not sure what was at the top of the hallway doors where we lived. When you reside amongst that many people and in that type of environment, it doesn't matter if you mopped the floors 3 times a day or bleach the walls all day long. Mice and roaches took over the projects. It was creepy. Mice ran up and down the interior walls at night as I slept in my bed. You could hear them scratching the walls. This is one reason why I'm terrified of mice today. Mother cleaned up the kitchen every night and never placed food on the stove because roaches literally took over the kitchen.

Coming from a cozy apartment in a three-family house, this felt like a dreadful nightmare. Turning on the kitchen light signaled all the roaches to scatter. I detested our living conditions. My Mother's goal was to get us out of the projects as soon as humanly possible, and she maneuvered her money to make that happen. It wasn't an easy goal to reach, especially while her husband lived as if he didn't have family to support. Mother's determination to give us a better life never leaves my mind. She demonstrated leadership qualities in my eyes. As we packed up our belongings on Morris Avenue, we knew that the projects would be a temporary living arrangement.

Mother furnished our apartment through purchases from the second-hand furniture stores. My bed was smaller than a twin bed. If I moved an inch too far, my butt would land on the floor. Never seen a bed that small in my life! Our furniture did not look like a typical living room set. By putting together different textures and colors, our living room looked presentable. Mother creatively worked her magic in our apartment. There wasn't a sound system or huge television to watch because we did not have cable. No plush carpet filled our bedrooms either. Mother worked to give us the simple things in life. Mother upheld the inside of the house and her personal appearance spotlessly clean. She was meticulous about the upkeep of the house. She taught her daughters to be domestic at an early age. It intrigued me to watch her cooking her favorite meals in the kitchen. Mother didn't write down any of her famous recipes. Just like Ma, Mother put a pinch of this and a pinch of that to make it taste delicious. My sister washed dishes and cooked the meals while Mother went to work. She combed my hair and made sure my clothes were neat and clean every day before leaving for school. Mother trusted her to look out for me. At picture-taking time in school, she combed my hair into cute, long ponytails and dressed me up in stunning dresses. There's one school picture that's still in my possession now that brings me back to those days.

The neighborhood was predominantly African-Americans. Most people worked while anxious to make ends meet. Although welfare was a part of this community, most parents went to work to earn a living. Some held several jobs because their household demanded more from them. Especially when the fathers were not around, the mothers had to fill the shoes of both parents.

A robbery in this community was second nature, especially around the first of the month. She insisted that I stay in the house after school. She was terrified of me playing outside in front of the buildings because of shootouts and robberies. While I didn't grow up in the projects, my neighbors easily engaged in conversations and became friendly with me. We stuck out like a sore thumb. The boys in my building tried to date me all the time because they were inquisitive to find out who was the new girl that lived on the 8th floor. When my family walked out of the building, we were gawked at from top to bottom. It was an awkward feeling. Most people that lived in the projects were born and raised there from childhood to adulthood. After living in the projects for two long years, we moved to a brand, new development and it felt great! My mother kept her promise to get her family out of the projects. Surely, I didn't miss living in the projects; however, the friendships with people that I met there can never be replaced. Back then, it felt as if we moved over one hundred miles away, but in fact, our new apartment was only two blocks away from the projects.

Today, those projects have been torn down and replaced with affordable townhouses. No more projects. That space has allowed people to rent and own property.

LIFE LESSONS:

Unfortunately, people who lived in the projects were looked down on. Let me say this, when Mother told me that we were moving to the projects, I thought – "Oh my goodness, are we going to be safe?" Of course, that is your first instinct when you're not familiar with that type of environment. Living there taught me to be familiar and mindful of my surroundings always, and how important it is to be humble to all situations. You never know what Allah has in store for you and which lessons He wants you to learn. Sometimes we think that we will stay on top and then one day, you're dropped down a few notches.

"Family, at times, could be your worst enemy. Just because they are family, we don't tell the truth to them out of honor. In the end, we are feeding into their destruction. Instead, tell them the truth, even if it hurts."

(Yasmeen Abdur-Rahman)

Chapter 4: Blood Is Thicker Than Water . . . Or Is It?

The older you get, the more you recognize that people who hurt you to the core, are the people with whom you share the deepest bond. Yes, that's right – I'm talking about family. Everyone goes through difficulties in their family, and my family is no different. It never ceases to amaze me at how 'brand new' people can get over material possessions. The relatives who were once like a sibling can turn out to be strangers. You wonder if you ever knew them at all. At first, you think "How could they have changed this much?" Then it hits you, and you realize that they are whom they always were and you're the one who has changed; not for the worse, but for the better. That doesn't lessen the pain of losing the close relationship that you once shared, but it helps you put things in perspective.

Justin and I grew up and socialized together like siblings! He and my other cousin who had the same name were so close. We planned and executed weekend gatherings and loved one another so hard. We could finish each other's sentences. You didn't see one without the other. We loved to sing together all the time. Music held us together. We got in trouble together. We didn't have much money to use, but we found ways to make each weekend adventurous. My childhood growing up with my cousins was the best!

Although we were close, I thought Justin was selfish. He was a taker and not a giver. Every conversation was about his feelings, who he was sleeping with, and what he looked like. He was openly Gay and flamboyant to the tenth power! He loved all the attention to be focused on him non-stop. His priorities were never about paying his car insurance or helping his Mother with the rent and utilities. His priorities were getting a pair of alligator shoes or a new, bright colored suit. Don't get me wrong, I love to look good, too but I wouldn't spend all my money on myself and put my family in jeopardy of eviction!

On Mother's Day in 2006, Justin called to wish me well. It was a nice gesture. During our conversation, I told him that my immediate family (Mother, son, sister, niece and nephews) and I were going to my mother's house for dinner. In my eyes, this was bonding time because we had been distant since I relocated to North Carolina. I expressed clearly to him that this gathering was for my immediate family only. However, his mother did not cook that day, so he believed it would be okay to join me anyway. Unfortunately, it took this incident for me to break out of my comfort zone with him. Although we grew up together, our lifestyles and religious differences were a world apart and our problems stemmed way beyond this incident. My relationship with my cousin ended that day. I wouldn't recommend anyone hold their emotions in for decades because once something major happens, there's no turning back.

During our conversation, it was obvious that I couldn't keep holding back on my 'real' feelings. For years, he portrayed himself as the victim. It's time to grow up, literally. Everyone seemed to constantly safeguard his feelings. When we were younger, he was in the special education classes. He acted unbalanced at times. Isn't it funny how people tend to motivate you to change your personality or opinions so that you're more like them on the outside? It's almost as if they want you to be the same person so that they aren't put in the spotlight for their own shortcomings.

Ultimately, my cousin should have checked his attitude and understood how he portrayed himself to others in public and to our family. We had never experienced an argument before, but at that time in my life, it wasn't healthy for me to continue to sugarcoat his issues only to make peace. It was time for him to grow up. At forty-six years old, he should have known better and wanted more for himself. It shocked him to the point that he was speechless.

My cousin didn't appear to think that something was wrong with his conduct. Unbelievably, he tried to turn the tables on me. He told the family that I was 'going through something' and that's why the argument ensued. Since he could not accept my honest opinion and did not like what I had to say, it was easier to classify me as crazy and deranged. He wasn't ready for the truth, and that took him out of his comfort zone. When I'm going through a dilemma, Allah is who I seek first then my friends or family are called on for secondary assistance. There will be times when I hear what they must say and disagree with it, but I respect their sincerity and then apply what works for me, personally, and take it from there. As they say, the truth hurts.

LIFE LESSONS:

Don't lose yourself in covering up your true feelings to safeguard someone else's ways. Be honest with yourself and others, all the time. When you try to make everyone else happy, you will find out that you're only hurting yourself. When you're speaking the truth, it will resonate and the other person will appreciate where your sincerity is coming from and accept or reject your thoughts and move forward.

My cousin and I recently began dialogue but it was short lived. Our closest cousin, who I mentioned earlier, passed away. Considering this devastating news, I decided to call him. This dreadful incident allowed me to say look 'let's move on and agree to disagree.' Instead, he answered by saying "I was waiting for you to apologize to me." Once again, his disconnect with reality was shaded by arrogance and pride. Everything that was expressed that day was articulated with honesty. For once in my life, I wasn't going to ignore my honest thoughts and feelings. He never called me again. My intentions, considering our cousin passing away, was to resolve our issues and continue to love each other. This incident taught me to express my true feelings because no one wants to be filled with false or fake love. We are family but we don't have to be friends. He lived with his mother his entire life, never moved out, not even once. In my opinion, it's pathetic, embarrassing and terrible for him to have lived off his mother as she prepared for retirement. She wouldn't move into a senior living apartment because she's too worried about her grown, adult son. How could anyone like this be taken seriously? Unfortunately, my cousin passed away. Instead of feeling sad for him, it led me to think back on all the good times we shared. He hid behind a great deal of chaos that people in our family overlooked, but as a Muslim, it didn't sit well with me. His lifestyle options weren't tasteful. Even in death, he's my cousin and I love and miss him.

"They say that money changes everything and that may be true. Then again, it can cause a separation in your family. Help those who need it and give because you can, not because people expect you to give."

(Yasmeen Abdur-Rahman)

"Too many people spend money they haven't earned, to buy things they don't want, to impress people they don't like."

Will Smith (Actor, Rap Artist and Entrepreneur)

"Riches are not from an abundance of worldly goods but from a contented mind."

(Prophet Muhammad) peace be upon Him

"Don't get attached to material things; get attached to your family."

(Author Unknown)

Chapter 5: Money Never Equals Happiness

The phone call that changed the lives of my family forever happened in the year of 2000. While sitting at my desk at work, Mother called with news that someone in our family hit the lottery. Her exact words were "One of your aunts' hit the lottery; she's a millionaire!" It was evident by the tone in Mother's voice that she wasn't as happy as she should have been with that newsflash. When you think about a family member becoming a millionaire, you would think that Mother was lost for words because she was overwhelmed with joy. Instead, she was disappointed.

I didn't know how to react. Initially, I thought, today is my retirement from corporate America. Well, here's where my story begins. After realizing that Aunt Bonnie won the lottery, my reaction to quitting my job quickly altered. It's like running into a brick wall with a dump truck. You can say that reality set in and retirement was not in my near future. It felt great thinking that my world could change. In my lifetime, I never thought anyone in my family would hit the lottery. It's that type of news you hear on television and read about in the newspaper. It felt like I should open the office door and shout the news to the entire office staff. There's a millionaire in my family!

Let me begin with the history of Aunt Bonnie. She's one of Mother's younger sisters. She worked in local bars and cleaned houses for a living. She has never had a corporate job. She didn't go to college or own a business. I am not sure if she graduated from high school. Aunt Bonnie wasn't a modest lady at all. She wore skimpy clothing. For example: dresses with slits up the back and sides or her breasts hanging out from the side of her dresses. She was, as they say, a party animal. She was loud and 'ghetto.' Aunt Bonnie's language was never professional. She cursed regularly. She yelled all the time.

As I reminisced through family photos, her photos reflect a bar setting or with different men. My Mother's siblings have various characteristics. My Aunt Ruby was the greatest auntie of all in my book. She passed away many years ago. She's in my thoughts all the time. Aunt Ruby was the backbone to the family. She said things that made you think. She was full of wisdom and fearless. She wanted you to be clear about what you wanted in life and then live it. She didn't take any nonsense from anyone!

All my mother's siblings worked hard to make it day by day. None of them grew up with a silver spoon in their mouth. Most were under-educated, poor and on welfare. None graduated from college and few barely made it out of high school or should I say elementary school. My mother's oldest brother, the only sibling who ran a business, passed away. They grew up in an era in Alabama where the children stayed home to help raise their siblings. All of them recognized what hard work was because at an early age they worked like adults without a salary. Picking cotton from the fields, cleaning up the house, and babysitting the younger children were tasks that girls from the south performed to help their parents. These actions forced the girls to grow up fast in the family. Most of them were married very young.

After Aunt Bonnie won the lottery, the next year, my son and I relocated to Cary, North Carolina. Most people at work assumed that my resignation from my position at Novartis Pharmaceuticals was due to the lottery money. Leaving Jersey, at my own free will, had nothing to do with my aunt's lottery winnings. If I thought that she had plans to support our family, trust me, leaving Jersey would never have crossed my mind. There was more out there in the world for my family and Jersey just wasn't cutting it. Therefore, our departure from Jersey left people, literally, thinking all types of thoughts. It was optimism that led me to think that Aunt Bonnie reserved a small portion of her winnings to support me comfortably in my new environment. It doesn't cost a thing to dream, right?

Since I knew Aunt Bonnie was not the 'giving' type of family member, the news didn't excite me as much as it did others. Most thought that she would take care of us financially, especially since most of our family needed monetary support. Some were unemployed, some were living with other family members, some were on drugs or suffering from chronic illnesses, and others had decent jobs that paid the bills. Most of our family, on Mother's side, were at least two paychecks away from being on welfare or homeless.

Personally, everyone thought she was going to, at least, go to her siblings and spread the joy throughout each family's household. That did not happen. It was my assumption that she would call her niece and say, "Hey, help me start and operate a business, because my money needs to be invested." She knew that I'm an entrepreneur and graduated from a business school. What better way to utilize my skills and keep the foundation growing in the family? As I said, most of my family was not educated. Using her money to start a business and invest was not one of her priorities. Instead, she continued to gamble in Atlantic City weekly and not invest her money. History has shown us that most lottery winners become homeless and broke after a few years. It's critical when you have that amount of money to make sure a team of advisors are set in place: lawyer, accountant, business consultant and religious clergy. Several family members with college degrees and exceptional experiences in corporate America would benefit from Aunt Bonnie's support. Immediately, I created a business portfolio for my aunt to view, but her son averted it in the mail. It never reached Aunt Bonnie. It would have been a blessing for Aunt Bonnie to become a venture capitalist for my business. With her support, there would be jobs for those who were unemployed in our family, but she wasn't concerned with any business ventures with me or anyone else.

Aunt Bonnie held the only winning lottery ticket and would live out the next 29 years of her life not worrying about anything. She would always have money, food, clothing, cars, homes, or whatever her heart desired. She's a true winner of prizes, jackpots in Atlantic City, Bingo and a host of other gambling environments. If you believe in luck or karma, it happened to her frequently. Mother thought that Aunt Bonnie was lucky growing up. No one was surprised when she hit the lottery. Aunt Bonnie was addicted to gambling. Since she was afraid of getting on an airplane, going to Las Vegas was out of the question. When she visited Atlantic City, she looked like an ordinary lady sitting in the VIP section. She didn't look like a millionaire at all. Her wardrobe placed her in the regular person category based on the

Capri pants, jogging suits and tee shirts. The first time I saw Aunt Bonnie dressed up extravagantly was a fur coat a few Xmas' ago.

She birthed four children: three of them are deceased and the last living son experienced jail and drugs. The oldest son, who recently passed away, was her right-hand son. He had a great deal to say about how my aunt's money was distributed. He was her lawyer, doctor, and banker. If he didn't like you, don't expect money or support. If he liked you, you'll receive a little here and a little there. Her son was concerned about supporting his non-related friends and people who don't have a bloodline to us.

Initially, the actions of her son disappointed me. While growing up, we were closer than his siblings. We sung together as if we were practicing for record deals. We shared secrets and acted out scenes to television and movie shows. We pretended to be superstars. We were protective of each other. We understood what it felt like to have and not have.

Before his death, my cousin sometimes acted as if we never met. Unquestionably, I knew that he would help me out financially. Instead, he never called, offered nothing in support, pretended to not have, or forgot where he came from and how hard it was to be poor. When we were in the same room together, there was an unspoken conversation going on. I looked at him and wondered where the love went but why money has taken us to a place where he doesn't care about me anymore? Despite the drama the money created, my love for him is forever. I wished one day, that he would call me and say that he was sorry for abandoning our friendship and family ties. That will never happen now since he's dead.

After relocating to North Carolina, I became unemployed and struggled to make my rent twice during that year. My mother suggested that I should call Aunt Bonnie. I got up the nerve to make the call. Every time I dialed her number, a second later, I put the phone back on the receiver. It was an awkward conversation speaking to a person that I grew up with and now I did not know how to begin my conversation with her. Since many people were calling for money, I never wanted her to think that money was the only reason why I was calling to speak with her that day.

She sent a money order to me for one-month's rent. It made me feel loved and appreciative. Once the money order reached me, I called Aunt Bonnie to thank her for the money and sent her a thank you card. Knowing that I wasn't calling to ask for money to shop, I would only call for serious reasons and paying rent is serious. Since Mother raised me to become independent, calling my aunt for help wasn't easy for me. My concept was that Aunt Bonnie would help me because I help myself.

Yet again, there was a desperate need to seek assistance, but this time Aunt Bonnie sadly surprised me with her response. My niece was on the other end of the line to witness her 'no' response. Aunt Bonnie wouldn't send the money because she claimed her pipes in her house needed fixing. Now, we're talking about a person who is a millionaire; how sad is that? As her niece, it felt like we were strangers. I felt like a figment of her imagination. Was this a dream? How embarrassing was this to tell my friends that I couldn't get another dime from the millionaire aunt?

I vowed that I would never pry into her life for anything else. Here is a woman that I grew up with and love unconditionally. Despite her money, we never had an argument or disagreement. We were extremely close. I remember when she lived in apartments with no food in her refrigerator. I took food from my house with me for the weekends. Growing up, I remember when her children needed a clean change of clothing. I remember watching her children use an iron to make cheese toast on the top of the stove.

No one in my immediate family should be destitute or struggling. No one in our family should be trying to figure out if they will have enough to eat today or if their lights will be shut off due to non-payment.

Every November for the next 29 years, Aunt Bonnie will cash a check for over a million dollars. How does she move forward in her spirit? Well, she continued to support one of her sisters. What amazed me is this sister, who she gave money to worked two full-time jobs, and her two, adult sons lived with her as well. Therefore, she had a substantial amount of income coming into her house monthly. Ironically, her bills were late and

Aunt Bonnie paid them every month.

My mother lived off a small, monthly social security check. Mother was in remission from battling Breast Cancer and volunteered at a local hospital for over 16 years. My mother supported everyone in our family; my aunt is no exception to this rule. There were times when Mother moved in her nephews when my aunts couldn't take care of them or needed support while they worked. My mother never said no to anyone in our family. There were times when several of her siblings occupied our living room floor as a place to sleep.

I love my aunt, rich or poor. My only wish is that she connected with our family. It's troublesome to think that our financial situations could be resolved in the blink of an eye. We assumed that life would be much easier to live. Her living son is kind and tries to help others with little of what he owns. He is friendly and considerate. After he was recently released from prison, we spoke on the phone. I told him that he must get himself together to conquer the drug war in his head. Our family is stressed to the maximum, but Aunt Bonnie sleeps every night comfortably.

At the beginning, my family was divided due to how Aunt Bonnie treated everyone. Just think how you would feel if you were struggling and a family member became a millionaire overnight. Aunt Bonnie resisted because she felt she's the only poor person growing up in our family under difficult circumstances. That is far from the truth. I guess it's what you say to yourself when you don't care. All her sisters were on welfare. All of them have children. Some have larger families than others. All grew up together. There was one year when at least four of the sisters were pregnant at the same time. We were a close family even at the poorest moments in our lives. Some of the aunts were married; all were either divorced or still married to their children's fathers. She had an angry disposition with the family. I'm still trying to figure out why to this day.

She stopped by periodically and gave us twenty dollars or more but nothing that allows you to live comfortably. Maybe two holidays in a row, she passed out money envelopes to the family. Some received the same amounts, but others, surely received more money if they were her 'favorites.' Unfortunately, one Xmas a family argument happened in the basement of her house. Two family members began to fight one another and it was a mess. This incident stopped everything for the family regarding Aunt Bonnie's support. Since that incident, the envelopes were more hush-hush or nonexistent. It's strange to wait once a year to get an envelope filled with less than a fast food restaurant paycheck. Most wait for that check with the hopes that it would be in an amount larger than the year before. Since she knew that her family needed help, why did she wait for that one day a year to give out an envelope?

When I'm around my aunt, I don't feel the closeness we shared while growing up. It's a weird type of feeling when we're around each other. For some reason, she visualized my sister as being the 'needy, abandoned sibling.' In her mind, I didn't require anything. My sister was one of her favorites and they were close. While my sister didn't have a high-paying corporate job or drove a new car, we both struggled in our own way. I wasn't a welfare recipient. I could use extra money to maintain my household. There is this crazy myth that Mother did more for me than my sister. Therefore, because of this insane belief, my support from Aunt Bonnie rarely happened. Because I was married with a good job, in her eyes, I didn't need any money. Because of my aunt's mentality, if you buy a new car, she thinks you're well off financially. If you buy a house, she knows that you are rich. These are normal purchases from people who are working, class citizens. Again, it's her ghetto mentality way of thinking.

Money doesn't change everything. Aunt Bonnie is overweight and feeling the pain of being a Diabetic. She could barely walk to her car without her knees throbbing of pain. She had a handicap parking sticker in her cars. Although she's over-weight, she could afford to hire a personal trainer or build a gym in her home. Even with all the money in the world, she's not happy.

In 2013, Aunt Bonnie had a massive stroke and a heart attack amongst other health-related issues. She's paralyzed on one side of her body. Where are those friends and family who she traveled with weekly to Atlantic City? Mother visited her in the hospital and at the nursing home daily and weekly. Every visit to Jersey, I visited her because it's the right thing to do. She looked healthier and tried to speak. She knows who you are but can't vocalize. I love my aunt. My prayer is that she makes it out of her illness. Perhaps, this test will prove to her that money doesn't totally make you happy. You get to see who categorically loves you when you're restrained in a hospital bed. Your family sits there and hold your hand; not the people who you take to Atlantic City to drink and gamble.

LIFE LESSONS:

In the end, Aunt Bonnie hit the lottery. She's the millionaire. It's her right to do with her money as she wishes. Unfortunately, others see the lack of support from her and it makes them feel sad, angry and disgusted. There's nothing we can do to change it now. Aunt Bonnie is bedridden and not of sound mind and body.

Many years have passed and we're all still poor, some middle class and others struggling as before. It's safe to say that she didn't have any plans to provide more than she has given to this date. Working comes naturally to me, so I'm content with what I have and what I've earned.

Overall, a person can do so much for their communities as well as their families. There are countless African-American colleges in the USA to support, and millions of homeless people, and children walking the streets with nothing to do. Once given the opportunity to give back, you should, all the time. Don't become inclusive of immediate friends and family only. You never know what the future has in store for you. Remember those you step on while moving on your way up, because they will be there to see you fall. I would rather be able to give than not give at all. In the end, she can't control anything about her life, even her money. The courts are managing her accounts and how her living arrangements are handled.

It's never too late to change. I hope Aunt Bonnie recovers from her illnesses. She should've talked to our family and resolved the issues instead of punishing us by not giving. That's the irony of life, you don't know what will happen from moment to moment. Never put money over your family or your life.

"There is space within sisterhood for likeness and difference, for the subtle differences that challenge and delight; there is space for disappointment and surprise."

(Christine Downing)

Chapter 6: Sisterhood

This is a chapter that I debated writing, but it's necessary.

At first, growing up with my sister was good for me, but aggravating for her. With such a huge age difference, the sight of me was her pain in the butt. Mother demanded that my sister watch over me while she worked a day and night job.

Since Mother wasn't home most of the time, she played the motherly role in her absence. When my sister invited company over to the house, mainly boys, my abilities to recall every detail to Mother kept her giving me long stares. My sister hated me witnessing things that weren't supposed to be known to Mother. We were 10 years apart.

When my sister had her first child, my niece, I was in middle school. My niece was and still is the apple of my eyes. She was the cutest little baby to me. When she slept, I would stand right in front of her crib and stare at her for hours. We're closer to each other than my sister and I are even today. They abruptly moved to Connecticut and that's where my nephew was born. Ironically, my nephew is 10 years younger than my niece.

By the time I graduated from business school in 1985, my sister became closer to me. Closer in the sense that we found more in common. We shopped together. We attended family gatherings together. After my ten-year marriage ended in divorce, we started going out to clubs together. We loved house music. House music is a popular type of music genre in Jersey. Because my family meant the most to me, it was a constant planning of weekend outings. At that stage of my life, my family was first priority over everyone. It became my motivation to make sure my immediate family was financially and emotionally good.

Sadly enough, I put a lot of pressure on myself to fill my dads' financial responsibilities to our family. When my sister needed financial support, without hesitation, a trip to an ATM machine to withdraw money was normal. It was from the kindness of my heart. It was never asked of her to repay back the money. Since she didn't have a license or car, it was natural for me to pick-up or drop-off my sister when she needed to go to the grocery store or laundromat. When times became harder for her with her children, she needed a place to stay. Without a second thought, my house became her residence. My sister never said thank you for all the times she moved in with me or for anything for that matter. Thank you just isn't in her vocabulary. Her arrogant and prideful nature made me feel guilty when I couldn't accommodate her requests.

Then my relationship with my sister took an unexpected turn for the worse. After vacationing with a close friend in North Carolina for two weeks, I came back to Jersey to announce my relocation to North Carolina. My sister's attitude changed and our sisterhood hasn't been the same. The question was, "Why do you want to move to North Carolina?" It wasn't a happy reply at all. Nor was it a response of happiness that I wanted to move on to another state with my son. It wasn't looked upon as a place to go and have fun with my sister. My sister has never said "I'm proud of you" or "I love you" or "thank you for being a good sister."

My sister stopped calling me. From the day that my son and I relocated to North Carolina in 2001 until now, my sister has never visited. When I talked to Mother, I asked her every now and again – "Did you speak to your other daughter today?" Mother would say, "No, it's been a while." Her response led me to believe she wasn't visiting or calling our mother as promised.

Prior to my relocation, my sister and I had a conversation about Mother. Mother was my concern while I was making my decisions to leave Jersey. For example, right before my high school graduation, my guidance counselor lined up several out-of-state colleges for me to visit. It was hard for me to get excited because there was a fear of leaving Mother alone in Jersey. Although our entire family lived in Jersey, to me, she would be alone. Most of them, just like my sister, rarely visited. Part of me wanted to enroll for college at the University of Connecticut which is in the state where my dad lived.

We agreed to give Mother money on a monthly basis. She agreed to spend at least one weekend at Mother's home. Since leaving Jersey, Mother and I spoke every day or every night. My sister is a Licensed Practical Nurse (LPN) at a local hospital. She takes care of elderly patients. She had contracted live-in jobs as well. To care for the elderly but not visit or give attention to your own mother made me angry. Mother said to me one day – "I almost forgot that I have another daughter." However, when I moved back to Jersey due to the unfortunate economy slump in North Carolina, my sister never offered a hand to help me. My BFF from elementary school invited me to stay with her for as long as necessary. She wouldn't accept money for her kindness. A true friend or family will not punch you while you're down. If my BFF wouldn't have stepped up, there weren't any other options. My son and I could've been homeless.

At the beginning of my move to North Carolina, it became hard to find permanent employment. Working temporarily became the norm to most people in the area due to the closing and relocating of companies in Research Triangle Park. Not once did my sister call me to offer help. Not once did my sister call to say that I love you. Not once did my sister send me a food package or offer to pay a bill while I was down on my luck. It's one of the saddest moments in my life. How could you not help your only sister? How could you talk about me to other people as if I am nobody to you? When I was helping out my sister, it felt like we were switching roles because she is the older sister. It's demeaning and embarrassing to have a sister who doesn't love or care about my circumstances. To live in North Carolina since 2001 and never show up or call to help me is unforgiving. How could this be possible? I keep asking myself – "What have I ever done bad to you to make you treat me this way?"

It's no secret that my dad and sister discussed me in a negative light. Strangely enough, when I do good, they don't say anything or congratulate me at all. Going through a bad economy didn't only affect me, it touched a lot of people. Where's the support instead of passing judgment on how you think I should live my life? They spoke regularly about why I should've stayed in Jersey with my good job in corporate America. Again, they missed the point of being supportive and saying encouraging thoughts. Yet, my sister had to get on welfare with no husband

and living from place to place. My family supported her but talked about me. For example, I purchased a brand new 2018 Toyota Corolla. When my dad called, it was the first thought in my mind to tell him of my new car. He started off with a negative comment. He talks to me as if I am a crackhead or someone who has a reputation for making bad decisions. Why is it okay for my sister to need help, but if I need help, it becomes the talk of the town? He holds me to a different set of standards.

Within two years, I was hospitalized for two major surgeries. Outside of a few other immediate family members, my husband was the only family supporting me. Since Mother was getting up in age, she didn't like the trips that involved driving to North Carolina. Instead, Mother called around the clock to check-up on me constantly. Any type of communication about my situations came through my niece. My niece communicated what my sister said about me, but my sister never calls me. She makes negative comments all the time. During those moments when it is normal for family to call or visit during an illnesses or surgeries, my sister who is a LPN didn't call or visit. Every year on her birthday, I reached out to her but she ignored me. Not once does my sister call, text, visit or send a card for my birthday. It's difficult to understand what has gone wrong with us because she won't talk to me. My family says that my sister became introverted and distant after Mother announced she was pregnant with me. Since she was the only child for so long, the shine was off her and landed on me. How many more excuses could you give someone who's almost retirement age?

We're totally opposite: skin complexion, height, profession, hobbies, marital status, careers and the list doesn't stop there. Even with all of those differences, we look alike, and born to the same parents. We share the same bloodline but I felt like her step-sister for most of my life.

Prior to the passing of Mother in April of 2017, we didn't communicate for decades. How sad is that for sisters? The day that Mother passed away, there wasn't any type of communication between us. It's interesting because I was on the phone with my uncle when the doctor told us of her passing. My sister was not the first call on my mind to make to my family because she's not emotionally connected to me or our mother.

When I arrived in Jersey, I expected some type of communication from my sister. Our mother is dead. She never reached out to invite me to her house. Since being a people-pleaser is in my DNA, reaching out to her was a typical reaction. Even when the family met up at Mother's house to compose her obituary, it was awkward for me. To get a hug, kiss or love from my sister would've changed my life. My dad was not there to support me.

The day of the funeral arrangements, she sat in the corner with nothing to say to me. Yet, months prior to Mother's death, Mother was admitted into alcoholic treatment. While my mother was in treatment, my sister was responsible for making sure her household was taken care of by paying her bills. She paid everything except her life insurance. My mother paid her bills on time. That's the same life insurance policy since I was a little girl. How could my sister not pay her life insurance? Yes, let the cable shut off but not her life insurance. Now, Mother is dead and we're scrambling to pay for her funeral. Mother was proud to have a life insurance policy for burial because she wasn't afraid of death. Mother talked about how she wanted to be buried many, many times during our conversations. My sister dropped the ball. She knew the family was upset with her for not paying Mother's insurance policy while she was in the hospital. Some of my family spoke out about it and they were upset. Who could blame them?

During the Wake and funeral, people were handing envelopes to my sister. My mother's co-workers didn't physically know me. They knew of me from conversations with Mother because she told them that her youngest daughter lives in North Carolina. The hospital where Mother volunteered gave my sister a huge envelope. My sister didn't split any monies with me or even address the envelopes that she received. At the time of Mother's death, I was working nights and my hours at work were cut. I was struggling to make ends meet. My cousin purchased a ticket from Amtrak to get me to her funeral. My sister was aware of my financial issues. How selfish could anyone be with their sibling? It took me a little time to understand why people who gave cards directly to me specifically said that the cards were for me only. It became clear that they knew more about my sister's behaviors with Mother than I did for sure. She didn't care how I was getting to Jersey or back home to North Carolina. Her actions confirmed what was on my mind already. It would never ever had been a thought that she wouldn't share what was given for Mother's passing with me. Boy, was I wrong about my sister. I should've spoken up to her but I avoided confrontation. That's a huge regret on my part. One day, we'll have that conversation and it probably won't go well.

My cousin and BFF opened their homes for my husband and I to stay with them. It felt uncomfortable staying at Mother's house. We stayed there for maybe one or two nights. My sister showed no compassion towards me during my visit to Jersey. This isn't normal for siblings to lose their mother and not have a connection.

Growing up from elementary school to high school, my peers wouldn't believe that I wasn't an only child. They thought I was joking when mentioning my sister during the topic of discussions. It hurt my feelings to think that people didn't believe me. I never showed how unhappy I was feeling on the outside. My fake smile showed up and my heart was broken at the same time. No one could understand why my sister was not there for support; emotionally, financially or physically. There are no memories of her supporting me for any cause or event in my life. Some would say that my sister was jealous. It's hard for me to not to come to that conclusion. Is it jealousy that I landed a lucrative corporate job, purchased several new cars, graduated from business school, relocated to another state and got married? Some would say that she was jealous of my relationship with both my parents. My family members don't understand my sister. They would say, she doesn't give out her number and address to them. If you manage to get her number, she avoided your call. She has been standoffish not only with me but our entire family.

To see my sister cry and fall over the casket at my mother's funeral was bizarre. No, I'm not saying that she didn't love her, but her actions towards Mother were suspect. She had opportunities to share love for our mother. By living in Jersey, she could plan time with Mother. Mother needed her to support her. She needed her to protect her from everyone who said terrible things about her in our own family. We sat separately at both the Wake and funeral. I thank Allah that my husband was there to support me the entire time and throughout my time back in North Carolina.

It's sad because as I think back to my time growing up in Jersey, even my nephews are distant with me today. Is it a family curse? I reached out to my nephew through social media and he doesn't respond. I believe that my sister's attitude and selfishness has passed down to them. They probably sat in the same room and heard how my sister feels about me over phone calls with my dad. It's sickening because I love my family so much. I have gone beyond to support my family. Where I live shouldn't be a negative, however, it should be a good thing. My house should be a get-away for my sister. Once my sister's kids became adults, our relationship as sisters, should be measured as BFF's.

I felt like the only child my entire childhood and adulthood. Being around friends who have siblings and show so much love to one another makes me wish I was a part of their families. They travel together, communicate on a regular basis and constantly say how much they love each other. My friends became my sisters. I called my BFF's and they comforted and supported me. My dad avoids any mention of my sister when we talk over the phone. My sister and dad are close today but were distant years ago.

As my memory goes back to the early eighties, it makes me believe that as long as I was giving or doing for my sister, we were good. When I could no longer support her financially, she disowned me. Looking back today, it's like she used me.

I keep going back for more punishment. Why should I feel guilty when good things happen for me? I continue to reach out to my sister. In 2018, I wrote her a letter, purchased a nice birthday card and texted her. No response. In Islam, you're not supposed to cut the ties with your family. When I say that I have given up, it means that I will no longer extend myself to her nonsense. If she desires a relationship with me, it will happen on her terms. My feelings have been hurt too many times. It's time to worry less about her and more concerned about myself. Now that Mother has passed away, my focus will continue to be on my son's well-being, the family who loves me, my close friends and my husband.

LIFE LESSONS:

The death of Mother changed my life forever. Her death taught me to stop trying to please everyone else to the point that I can't focus on my own happiness. Stop chasing a dream and deal with the reality that's in front of me. I learned that what you give to other people and how you treat them doesn't reflect how they treat you in return. Some people take for granted a person who is kind and loving. A person like me is taken for granted because I wear my heart on my sleeves. I've been an emotional person since a young age. When I love, I love hard. When I care for you, it's loyalty to the end. For me, it about helping others and being supportive in order to make sure the people you love aren't suffering in any way. My sister is selfish. She is heartless. Observe the people who don't have close friends. Observe those who can't stay in solid and stable relationships that progress to marriage. Observe people who don't socialize with their families. Observe people who only take but never give. Observe people who never have anything good, motivating, or positive to say about people who progress at different stages of their lives. Observe people who can't tell you how they feel about you. Especially observe women who do not have a loving relationship with their mother. I could only guess that there are things that happened to my sister which do not personally pertain to me but if you don't talk about it, it won't just go away. When you harbor things that happened to you or emotions that you do not express, you become an unhappy person. I feel like the hatred that my sister has for me is based on nothing that I did to her personally. It has most to do with the fact that I exist; I was born. People say that when a child endures another brother or sister many years later, they tend to show animosity towards that sibling. Maybe one day she will open up to me. Maybe one day she will call or visit me and express her feelings. Maybe one day she will be that loving sister that I've desired to have in my life. Maybe one day she will be the shoulder I need to hug or cry on when I'm missing our mother.

Although I'll be happy without her, she's a huge empty space in my life that no one could replace. It's time for me to stop talking about why my sister doesn't love me. It's time for me to love on the people who show love for me no matter what's in my bank account, my place of residence, what type of car I drive or if I work for a big corporation. None of those things matter when you love someone unconditionally. My love for my sister is unconditional despite how badly she treats me. While my mother's death hasn't stopped me from crying, it feels like my sister is dead, too.

"We learn about gratitude and humility – that so many people had a hand in our success, from the teachers who inspired us to the janitors who kept our school clean ... and we were taught to value everyone's contribution and treat everyone with respect."

(Michelle Obama)

Chapter 7: School Days

My mother enrolled my sister and me in public schools when we were little girls. As my memory would serve me, my demeanor in school was that of a quiet, bright and creative student. As a well-liked child, I went four whole years of elementary school without having any problems with anyone . . . that's until Kathy Thomas decided to make it her personal mission to make my life miserable. Her face sticks in my mind like a sore thumb! I never figured out why, but for whatever reason, she despised me. She sat behind me in English class. She pulled on my long ponytails and threw candy paper on my desk. She commented that I thought I was cute and smart.

Kathy was not one of the popular girls in school. The acne on her face was atrocious. Even at that age, she harbored hatred in her heart and her face never wore a smile. She and several other girls wandered around the school daily just to terrorize other students. Until writing my memoirs, I wondered what happened to Kathy. Maybe she found happiness with her life and peace in her heart. Looking back, perhaps her actions reflected things that happened in her life.

Unlike most of my friends and fellow classmates, school was a big deal to me. Mother placed education as a high priority for her children. I didn't want to disappoint her or my dad. I excelled in many classes. Typing was my favorite subject. As an exceptional typist, I won countless awards in elementary school. While spending a summer vacation with my dad, one of my requests for back to school supplies was a typewriter. As I've mentioned before, my dad was "tight-fisted" with his money. Getting a dollar from him was a huge project. Once again, his girlfriend Edith came to my rescue. She could not believe that he would deny me this one gift, especially knowing that I was an "A" student in school. She made a good argument on my behalf, and finally, he gave in and we traveled to Sear's to purchase the typewriter. This moment brought happiness to me. Anxiously I waited to take it home to show Mother after summer vacation was over.

By the 4th grade, my typing instructor, who just so happened to be a Muslim, became a huge role model for me. She took me under her wing, and I excelled under her tutelage. While attending her class, it became evident to me that typing was my passion and she was in my life for many reasons. She recognized me as one of her top students and secretly doted on me. Some students envied our relationship, but I didn't pay them any attention. As her student, we continued to build a strong bond and she became a mother figure in my life. Since we both practiced the same religion, we attended events together.

One day, I began to ache after coming in from jumping rope in gym or from something as simple as running up and down the street. My entire body felt like fire! The pain felt as if it would never go away. My hands, shoulders, arms and legs would swell and none of the over-the-counter medications relieved the pain. By touching my body, you felt the heat of the fever of my inflamed joints. It's like walking on hot, burning coals. My parents made an appointment for me with a cardiologist and rheumatoid arthritis specialist. Both doctors diagnosed me with a heart condition called Rheumatic Fever. Most people didn't know what this meant in terms of my health, but my doctors described it to me as a fever around my heart. The aches and pains were the beginning symptoms of this awful disease. While in the 6th grade, the disease began to flare up on a regular basis. One day, while at school, the severity of it caused the school nurse to call my parents. They quickly rushed me to the hospital. I spent weeks as a patient in the Intensive Care Unit of Saint Barnabas Hospital in Jersey. After the doctors released me, they insisted that a private tutor come to my house to get me caught up on my lessons for school. After a year of tutoring at home, most students thought that I would not graduate with the class. The students were surprised when I walked across the stage, with honors, no less to receive my diploma. This illness would creep up on me from time to time when I was stressing about something. When stressed or an extreme cold or rainy day, my health changed without warning. Without Penicillin, Amoxicillin and Advil, the pain didn't go away for at least a week or longer.

Because of my health issues, my time and efforts went

into performing well in my academic studies. Gym and other physically demanding classes were no longer an option for me in school. I began to steer towards the business curriculum. Maintaining an "A" average was vital to me. My parents were happy to see my report card each marking period. They grew up without an extended education, but they wanted me to keep my focus on school. They knew what they lacked was what I needed to build and improve my life in the future and for my future children. My name consistently showed up on the honor roll listings. Watching my mother's face light up when she saw all the A's on my report card, was like watching an Alvin Haley Dance performance. Her excitement of me brought tears to my eyes. I remembered listening on the other phone while she would tell her friends and other family members that her daughter made her proud.

Once I made it to high school, I thought I had it all figured out. As a freshman, right away, I signed up for business-related courses. I loved the whole idea of attending business classes because in my opinion, these classes made me think outside the box. I took Accounting, Typing, Stenography and other business-related subjects. Additionally, my participation in business competitions allowed me to show off my typing skills. I won several awards and acknowledgements throughout high school, including having my name on a listing in a nationwide scholastic directory for exceptional achievers.

In high school, everyone paid attention to what you wore and whom you were dating. The girls were rude and jealous, if you looked halfway decent. There were many cliques walking around and gossiping about things that were not important. The most popular girls hung out together; the smart crew was together and the least likely to be popular were together. While browsing through my high school yearbook, it's indescribable how so many people were on point with their future predictions. Unfortunately, many students who became adults died at an early age, some are successful and others are walking the streets of Newark in a daze.

In 1984, after graduation from high school, I decided to attend Drake College of Business in Elizabeth, New Jersey. Going to business school provided courses necessary to further my corporate and business career. Because of my spectacular grades, going to a 4-year college was an option, but I didn't want to leave my mom. This decision began the start of how my life moved positive for me. I achieved a business/word-processing diploma a year later. When I initially expressed to Mother that I signed up for business school, she was troubled that on a financial level, this goal wasn't achievable. Nonetheless, I reassured Mother that I would pay back the loan, and my promise to her was achieved. Furthering my education made my parents, once again, proud of me. Many of my family members did not graduate from high school or college so, of course, this achievement affected all of us. My mother, grandmother and aunts attended the award ceremonies. This was the only time I remembered receiving support from my extended family; I'll never forget that day.

After attending business school, I decided to go to Union County College in Cranford to take additional business courses with the hopes of getting my BA in Business Administration. Going to college at night was a bit challenging because my son allocated my time at home while working a full-time job. Trying to study and complete homework assignments during my lunch hour at work became a challenge, too. Relaxing and finding time for me was null and void. I felt the pressure of succeeding in a world where, at the time, flexibility and assistance for single parents was not as important as it is today. Although Mother continued to support my endeavors, GOD had another plan for me.

LIFE LESSONS:

As you can probably tell by now, education and my thirst for knowledge tie into every aspect of my life. Growing up, there was a passion to pick up a book to read and still today, you can catch me in a local Barnes and Noble bookstore. I have a huge love for books. Reading the newspaper, a magazine or a novel helps you to learn more about what happens in the lives of others and the state of affairs around the world. I advised my son that he should read more but realized that he only followed the requirements of him in school. In my mind, I wanted him to go to the bookstore with me and have that same enjoyment that I felt when walking through the doors. Not everyone will go to college and perhaps it's not for everyone. Going to college requires focus and motivation. You must feel that it will benefit towards whatever goals you choose. My parents never pushed me towards college. They said that it was my decision and my life. They felt that I would succeed in whatever it was that I had a passion for in life. Whether it was going directly to a 9 to 5 or pursuing a college degree, they supported me. It's not a wrong or right choice; it's a choice that you must make for yourself and not for your parents.

I have noticed today that most parents are telling their kids that they 'must' go to college. In my opinion, that is a recipe for disaster. It's best to sit down with your children first to hear what their thoughts are about their lives and ambitions. The worst mistake a parent makes is demanding their children go to college. If it's not a goal that they plan to reach, allow them the space to find their way. Between 18 and 25 years of age, most kids are not sure what to do first. Parents should be supportive and less demanding, especially when your children have so many obstacles to tackle every day in their circle. Remember how you were engaged in peer pressure? It's worse for them today. We, as parents, cannot live out our dreams through our children. It's not acceptable. If you went to college and achieved three degrees, that does not mean your children will follow the same path.

My advice to kids in high school today is to maintain excellent grades. If you do not have transcripts with all A's or passing grades, get help from your guidance counselors immediately and from your peers. Maintain a progressive relationship with your guidance counselor. Explore all your options. Think outside of your surroundings. Even if that consist of traveling outside of where you live to other states for college – explore. Seek a mentor. Find someone who is working in the job or business that's your passion. Take advantage of scholarships and grants. Focus aggressively on furthering your education by way of a 2-year or 4-year college, technical, trade or business school.

Prepare yourselves for a world outside of high school. Do not engage in drugs or unprotected sex. Be patient with your parents because they have come from a place of knowledge and experience. Always respect your parents or any adults, for that matter.

On the other hand, become a business owner. Create an opportunity for yourself and your community. We should discuss this option with our children. My parents under no circumstances talked about entrepreneurship. Now that I am a business owner, I see the importance in it for our communities. This avenue helps others in your community prosper as well. It opens doors to employ people in your community.

Although it may seem effortless to find a job at McDonald's or Burger King, it's not going to give you the experience you will need to work in corporate America. Financially, it takes longer to establish a nest egg to purchase a home, a car or advance to your next level. The same goes for retail jobs; easy to get in but harder to switch gears once you're in it. Always remember where you come from because success could be temporary.

"A mirror reflects a man's face, but what he is really like is shown by the kind of friends he chooses."

(Unknown Author)

"Friendship is the hardest thing in the world to explain. It's not something you learn in school. But if you haven't learned the meaning of friendship, you really haven't learned anything."

(Muhammad Ali)

"A friend is a friend when you two share a common denominator: religious obligations, moral characters, and true integrity. Look at the people whom you call friends. Do they fit that criteria? Trust me, a friend could steer you to Heaven or Hell. Be careful who you call a friend."

(Yasmeen Abdur-Rahman)

"Your friend is the one who tells you the truth, not the one who simply agrees with you, and your enemy is the one who simply agrees with you."

(Shaikh Muqbil)

Chapter 8: What About Your Friends?

According to the American Heritage College dictionary, the word 'friend' means a person who one knows, likes, and trusts; a person whom one knows, an acquaintance; a person with whom one is allied in a struggle or cause; a comrade. One who supports, sympathizes with, or patronizes a group, cause, or movement.

To Muslims, our 'friends' are called Companions. To me, a friend is irreplaceable in your life. I've met scores of astonishing people during my lifetime. It's a breathtaking opportunity to converse with people from other countries, ethnicities, religions, cultures and businesses. Some have strengthened and weakened my friendship base.

The United States is a melting pot full of every nationality, culture and religion. As an adolescent, my usages of the word "friend" tend to be used lightly. Every other week, a new friend came in my life. You can say that back at that point, it became obvious that my personality somehow made me a people-pleaser. Putting a smile on everyone's faces remained my sense of duty in school. It's easier to fit in if you're likable or looked up to. Maturity taught me that not everyone you meet is a friend. Certainly, not everyone has your best interest at heart.

It's shocking how you meet someone, and within a short timeframe of your life, you become so attached that you begin to share all your private and intimate details. This person allows you to open up and be yourself in public and in private. In middle school is where I met one of my best girlfriends, Brooke. We were as thick as thieves, and if you saw one of us, you knew the other was not far behind. Our friendship today is just as solid as ever 30 years later, and that's the example of a 'true' friendship.

With a real friend, you're completely candid with your difference of opinions, your viewpoints and your actions. You're at no time self-conscious with whatever you say. You don't concern yourself with perfect grammar. You're not worried if you use the correct utensils while at dinner. The words out of your mouth exit freely and without hesitation. When you're amongst friends or companions, they recognize your feelings. It's not from a phony person chatting to someone that you don't know. When you are friends with someone, there must be sincerity and honesty. When you lie about what you're feeling, how can you be a friend? A friend should never feel like she should overlook a topic or issue just to make you content. A friendship shouldn't feel like torture. People say that I'm honest and sensitive with my words and actions. Therefore, in living with my personal characteristics, honesty with my 'friends' is top priority for me.

Growing older allows me to realize that it's not about how many times you see your friends; it's about the quality of time you share. It's important to know they have your back when you need them. It doesn't give me anxiety if we don't talk each day. It does trouble me if my friends miss important dates or events that take place in my life that pertains to my personal or business affairs. Support should be reciprocated and set as a priority in your friend's lives. Everyone has a diverse life at home, but a friend is family to me. My friends aren't expected to make me their number one priority. What is expected from a friend is their honesty and unconditional love. A friendship goes both ways and you get back what you put out. It's not about how much money you have or what type of home you live in that makes us friends. Today, my friendships are spiritual in nature. We experienced similar circumstances or we're traveling in the same direction based on business, religion, or delicate situations.

A few times during my life, it became necessary to 'release' people that I thought were my friends. Ending a friendship, in some cases, has the same conclusion as ending a marriage. It will either work and grow or continue with resistance. When the two ends don't meet, there begins the headaches and tensions. I remember vividly how one ex-friend continuously judged others and their state of affairs. She acted arrogant and materialistic. Some people whispered they didn't understand why we were friends in the first place. My personality and spirit love and cares for others, with little sarcasm. My close friends thought it seemed bizarre, to say the least, that she became my friend. As I've reflected and taken stock of how the relationship ended, it's understandable where they were coming from at that time in my life. At first, my blinders were on and my blindness to my relationship with her changed my personality or the true me in the inside. I'm surprised that I allowed this to continue for so many years.

The ex-friend invited me to an all-expense paid visit to Jersey and I unexpectedly had to dig deep in my pockets to clear up her mess. She disrupted my household and put me in financial madness that placed me further in debt. At the end of that visit, she promised that she would put the money that I dished out for the trip into my checking account. I called to remind her about the money she owed to me. She made a commitment to me and didn't come through as promised. She knew that I was unemployed, at the time, and struggling financially. Eventually, she put a 'few dollars' in my account but she acted as if I was bothering her. Is this how you treat your friends? At that point, there was no doubt in my mind that I needed to end this stressful, one-sided friendship. It felt as if I wasted so much of my time relating to her when I knew her ideas were poison. I felt like a fool when she put me in that situation. Why did she commit herself and act as if she was able to support me? When in fact, she was financially in trouble and overextended herself. She wanted me to believe that everything was great in her life. As a friend, she should have been 'honest' with me instead of being deceitful.

Another unpleasant incident happened to me. A friend who I've known since high school called me one night. She said the reason why she was calling me was to give me an ultimatum. She proclaimed that if I don't call her next she doesn't plan to be my friend any longer. At first, I thought she was joking. At that moment, I comprehended that an adult came at me as if we were children playing at the playground. Then I realized that she was serious because the phone line got quiet.

After taking in what she said over the phone, I finally replied to her demands: "You can't put a timeline on when I must call you. If we're friends, it doesn't matter if I call tomorrow, a month from now or once a year. You live in Jersey and I live in North Carolina. I'm married and you're single. We are not the same two people from high school. A friendship should be unconditional and without limitations."

Honestly, our friendship went south when I relocated to North Carolina. She dreamed of relocating to the south, but all her friends relocated first. She was the last of the group that remained in Jersey. Her anger was misplaced and it should never have gotten to the point where our friendship ended. She unfriended me from her Facebook page. Her gesture made me laugh on the inside because it felt as if we were complete strangers. The negativity and judgments displayed in previous conversations were constantly going against the grain.

From time to time, you may come across people who seem sincere. They tend to be on the phone with you but there is a one-sided conversation going on. They don't allow you to speak before cutting your sentences short to finish off their thoughts. Their issues are persistently more significant than yours. You feel out of touch with this person. It's my understanding that true 'friends' are not narrow-minded people. There were many times when a friend called with devastating news regarding spousal problems or job issues and required my advice or needed a friend's support. Often, it's better to listen and not say a word. It's not beneficial to their frustrations or hurt to antagonize their troubles. Be a friend. See beyond your needs for a split second. Go to their house to give them a hug, send a card or just say, "I love you' and if you need anything, I'm here for you.

This chapter can't be completed without mentioning a special friend, Tasha. She and I met while we both lived in an apartment complex on Prince Street in Jersey. She lived across the hall from us and when we were hanging out together, it was so much fun. We would order food, or just sit at her kitchen table and talk about everything and laugh all night. Her friendship is special because we find amusement, laughter and joy with every telephone call or visit with one another. She makes me smile even when my heart is broken or when we're just sitting on the telephone. She and I say the funniest things when we talk to one another. She's one of those friends who you just can't stay mad at and even when we disagree, in the end, it becomes a laughing matter. She has my back! When I need a pick-me-up, she's the friend that I call on speed dial.

If you're friends with someone and you're not honest with them, you're not a friend. If they ask you for advice and you say exactly what they want to hear, you're not a friend. If you try to downplay a situation to make it appear less damaging, you're not a friend; you're being friendly; there is a difference! Always have respect for someone else's thoughts. There are moments when I have differed with my friends, but that doesn't mean they are correct. It means that we're all individuals with individual opinions. We think and resolve situations in our own way. My circle of friends knows that I'll never deceive any of them nor will I take their love and friendship for granted. They trust that I'll keep their secrets and never let them down.

My phone book has been reorganized. It held names of people that were taking up too much space in my life. I understand now that it's not how many people you know, but the quality of those relationships that counts most. Now my phone book lists people who are compatible with me, religiously sound, going my direction, and positive. These people can count on me and we count on each other. Perhaps now, my ex-friends have looked back at the history of our friendship and can honestly see where they eliminated a perfect union. I wish the best for them.

To grow, you must know your strengths, weaknesses, and responsibilities. Change is hard. My fault was enduring the friendships knowing in my spirit that they were like horrible nightmares. I regret not being direct with my feelings. When you're dependent on a person, you will live in their shadow in order to keep them in your life. I believe "Madea" (Tyler Perry's character) said it best –

> "Some people come into your life for a lifetime and some come for a season. You should know which is which. I put everybody that comes into my life in the category of a tree. Some people are leaves on a tree. The wind blows, they go to the left. The wind blows from the other way they go to the right. They are just unstable. You can't count on them for nothing. All they ever do is take from that tree.

What you need to understand about a leaf is that it has a season. It will wither, die, and blow away. There ain't any need to be praying over a leaf to be resurrected. When it's dead, it's gone. Let it go. Some people are like that. All the leaf ever does is cool you off every now and then. If you're grown, you know what I'm talking about, because you can call them in the middle of the night and get cooled off. That's the leaf people. They come to take. Then there are people like a branch. You got to be careful with branch people. They come in all different shapes and sizes. You never know how strong they will be in your life. My advice is to tip out on it slowly. When you're going out on a limb, don't put too much weight on it at once, because it can fall and leave you high and dry. Sometimes, you must wait for a branch to grow up before it can hold all the things you want to share with it. Finally, there are like roots at the bottom of the tree. If you find two or three people in your entire lifetime that are like roots, then you are blessed. The roots don't care anything about being seen. All they are there to do is hold that tree up and to make sure it stays in the air. It comes from the earth to give that tree everything it needs. That's what relationships should be about – That's what you need; people who want to be in your life for the right reasons. If somebody wants to walk out of your life, you must let them go! When you learn to love yourself, you will end up giving standards to everybody around you. Again, I repeat for emphasis, if they don't meet your standards, you must let them go, because they might be a leaf. And forgive them with all your might." (Madea Simmons)

LIFE LESSONS:

Today, without hesitation, my friends identify with me better than my family. My friends connect to me emotionally, spiritually, religiously and mentally. My friends are on familiar terms with my personal life. My friends stay up in the dead of night with me when a decision needs to be concluded for work, business or in my personal life. My friends rally around to put a smile on my face when anxiety, depression or apprehension lurks into my existence. My friends are excited to hear when business is doing great and my goals are being met.

Surely, because I take this extremely serious, a handful of friends are exceptional to me. A few of them are entrepreneurs and talking about business is natural dialogue that we encounter on a regular basis. We think of ways to market our businesses. I cherish those times when we can talk candidly and know that our conversations are sacred.

If your friendships begin to make you feel agitated and uncomfortable, get out of that relationship. Stop and look at who you are and what you expect from your friends and the people in your circle. There are times when chaotic relationships are back into working order by default. If you're not honest with yourself, you're destined to bring the same type of people and energy in your life all over again.

Here are some thoughts that I have received from others in the past:

- On no account should you chat about your dilemma with people that are lacking ability of contributing to the way out of your problems.
- Those who never succeed themselves are always first to tell you how. Not everyone has a right to speak about your life.
- Don't give someone else the power to create your future. You'll receive the worst information when you exchange ideas with the wrong people.
- Do not follow anyone who is not going anywhere. If the path that they take leads to nowhere, go the other direction.

"Relationships are what make your life full. They keep you embedded in dialogue. Some relationships will enhance your life; others will tear down your spirit. Listen to your spirit and embrace only the relationships that make you laugh, not cry."

(Yasmeen Abdur-Rahman)

Chapter 9: Love, Lust, and Lies

While growing up, my parents (especially my dad) were strict. He is a member of the Nation of Islam (NOI). In fact, my parents banned me from dating until I reached the 12th grade, and at the time, it seemed so unfair to me because my girlfriends were dating. It felt like being out of the loop. If I had known then what I know now about relationships and all the drama that comes with them, waiting would have been my priority.

Eddie Burwell was my first boyfriend and first love. Eddie was quite handsome. His hair was curly and brown. He had a light red mustache, which was a unique trait on an African-American male in our neighborhood. Eddie's parents get credit for raising him to be a well-mannered, shy and soft-spoken young man. As I have said, my parents prohibited me to date until the 12th grade – so that meant that I had to be creative … in other words "sneak" around to be with him.

At the time, Eddie and his mother lived in the Vailsburg section of Newark. Each weekend, I lied to Mother about going to one of my girlfriend's houses to hang out or study. I took a bus across town to meet Eddie. We went on long walks in the park or to the movies every single weekend. His mother approved of our relationship. I remember thinking that she was a "cool" Mom who was the opposite of my mother. She didn't ask questions about our relationship. She was okay with him dating me. It never occurred to her that I was breaking my mothers' rules by dating her son. His mom probably thought that dating was natural at our age.

Once I entered the 12th grade, it was okay to let the secret out about Eddie. When Eddie was invited to my house and family activities, everyone fell in love with him. When looking back on things, disobeying my parent's wishes was deceitful. When you're a teenager and the hormones are raging, no one can tell you that you don't know what's best.

Eddie was my date to my senior prom – no questions

asked. My gown was professionally handmade with exquisite silk materials in red with black trim. The sleeves were tapered close to my arms with huge cuffs with a long split in the back. My cousin worked in the shoe department of Bamberger's (known today as Macy's) in downtown Newark. She purchased a black and red stiletto heel pair of shoes for me, which matched my gown perfectly. Most girls dream of their senior prom day. It felt wonderful to dress up in this spectacular gown, wear flawlessly applied makeup (thanks to my cousin Denise) and drive up to the venue in a brand-new car (even if it was a rental).

At the time, Eddie did not have a valid driver's license. His dad drove us to the prom in a rental car. Afterwards, I drove us to the after party. The car was a white, two-door Chrysler with red, leather interior. When we stepped out of that car, you couldn't tell us that we weren't "Hollywood" – we were too sharp.

Prom was an enjoyable event for me. That day holds many memories that will remain embedded in my mind for the rest of my life. We danced the entire night and mingled with my classmates. We took pictures and ate a great meal, but unbeknown to Eddie, after the prom, my plan was to break up with him. Now, breaking up with someone after the prom may seem a bit cruel but I felt like my time with him didn't have a place in my plans. I set goals and began to prepare for my future, but that wasn't important to Eddie. He didn't make any concrete plans for his future after high school. As they say, he's such a mommas-boy! There wasn't any motivation in him. I searched beyond his looks and thought about where he would fit in my future. Eddie moved in life at a pace that was slower than a turtle moving around in the sand at a beach. I could not be held back like that because my ambitions were keeping me motivated to succeed.

The night that I broke off our relationship, Eddie took the news hard and demanded that we stay together as a couple. He became irritated and behaved completely opposite of the dude I had grown to love. He stalked me by hiding in bushes outside my house. Eddie called me on the phone excessively. When I began dating someone new, he shot out the windows of that dude's car. At first, I didn't know he did it, but his accomplice started talking about it to various people in the neighborhood and word got back to me. Once my new boyfriend found out who vandalized his car, he pressed charges and the courts subpoenaed me to testify against Eddie. This decision was hard for me to make, but it was necessary because here was a person whom I trusted with my life. I guess when you're in that type of jealous mental state you would carry out such a scary act. The streets of Newark took their toll on him. When I hear his name it's hard to believe that at one point in my life I saw this man as my husband and dad to my child. Recently, it was reported that he's working and looking like the old Eddie from high school. I'm so happy that he's a progressive citizen of Newark and holding down a good job.

My next serious relationship with a guy named Michael began about a year after I graduated from high school. We met while my girlfriend and I were out walking during the summertime of 1985. He drove by, saw me and turned his car around to talk to me. That was flattering, like something out of a movie to my 'young' mind. When he asked me out, I eagerly accepted his invitation. Michael was well-groomed, attractive, confident and self-assured. He was five years my senior. He seemed stable and mature, totally unlike my previous boyfriend; that made his stock value increase in my eyes. He was unexpected, but a welcomed change.

We dated exclusively for three years, and at the beginning of our relationship, he seemed like a 'dream' come true. He went out of his way to make me happy. On a weekly basis, he planned time with me even if it meant sitting with him on my couch watching a baseball game. The baseball games put me to sleep. In Michael's eye, we were spending 'quality' time together. He was a sweetheart. I was the happiest girl in the world! He found ways to take our relationship to another level. One of the most memorable moments in our relationship was when Michael planned a wonderful trip to the Bahamas for us. He planned everything. My job was to pack up my suitcase and be ready to go. He passionately loved to cater to my needs and the attention kept a smile on my face. Unfortunately, even though this relationship grew into something magnificent, Michael cheated on me with someone else shortly after we returned from our trip. He devastated my soul and disappointed me. I couldn't trust him anymore. Without trust in a relationship, it was time for us to go our separate ways.

Many years passed, but Michael would cross my mind from time to time. He met someone new. They created a little girl and my contact with Michael was gone. I assumed he became happily married, a family man – but in 2005, Mother called to say that she saw him while working at the hospital where she volunteered. She wondered if she could give him my contact information. Since I never stopped thinking about him, and wondering "what if," I told her it would be okay. A day or two after that, he called! We were both so happy to hear one another's voice that we kept interrupting each other. There were many things to talk about – catching up on old times, talking about our respective families and everything else in between. It amazed Michael that I remembered so much of our relationship, and how much of it he managed to delete from his thoughts. He apologized again for his transgressions and I accepted his apology. Most men would deny any wrongdoings, so I appreciated his mature gesture. From that day and for the next two months, we were on the phone with each other daily. I began to think that maybe we could rekindle our relationship. There was nothing to lose and much to gain. Plenty of time passed by, but we were both older and wiser now, and surely, we wouldn't make the same mistakes. He focused on wanting to be in a serious, committed relationship and said that infidelity of any sorts was no longer an option.

Since things were moving along so well, we made plans to spend 2006 Valentine's Day weekend together. We estimated that four months was a great 'catching up' period. We were now ready to see each other for the first time in years. Reservations and planning of my trip to Jersey was well on the way! As the Amtrak train moved closer to Newark Penn Station, my nerves began to shake my existence. The insides of my stomach-started summersaults, back flips and quickly knotted up! I didn't know what he looked like or if we would still be attracted to one another. On top of all that, the train was running late! Imagine adding that to a stressful situation. By the time the train arrived at Newark Penn Station, I was a wreck! I took a minute to breathe then called Michael to let him know I arrived safely. He pulled up within 15 minutes. When I saw him pull up in that shiny Beige Lexus, (Michael always believed in having a hot ride) I got butterflies all over again. I walked up to his car, trying to be calm, cool and collected. He grabbed my suitcase and gave me a big hug and kiss! WOW! It made me feel giddy and overwhelmed by his presence. I could tell that he was just as nervous as I was while he drove me to my mother's house. Although he's bald and gained a few extra pounds (let's face it, most of us are a little heavier than 20 years ago), he's the same person from my past. I remember saying to myself, "He still looks the same and the voice never changed."

We spent the entire weekend together. We went to the movies a couple of times and ate dinner at a few restaurants. It was breathtaking to hook up again with a man that displayed so much love for me. As in the early days when we were dating, Michael paid for everything that weekend and spared no expenses on food and entertainment. Michael continued his polite and well-mannered gestures by opening car doors for me. During one of our talks over dinner, he began to share his idea of how a woman should behave in a relationship. At first, I thought he joked a good deal when he said to me that the man has the last say in a relationship, but unfortunately, he was not joking. His facial expressions were serious and he didn't crack a smile. He made this same statement repeatedly during the entire weekend. I overlooked that and many other things that Michael said during our time together because of the excitement that I felt. The visit moved along according to plan. It felt too good to be true, but then the red flags began to wave. Michael dropped me off at my girlfriend's house to spend a few hours catching up with her. She and I were having so much fun together. Later that night, she dropped me back to Mothers' house. When I arrived at my mother's, I gave Michael a courtesy call. Although my intentions were simple and honest, he became angry when I called him, and this shocked me. I guess he assumed I was checking up on him, when in all honesty that was the farthest thing from my mind. It did make me wonder why he was so suspicious and defensive, but I decided to wait and see and not pass judgments. At the end of our visit, our goodbye felt awkward. It felt like all the feelings that I felt years ago were coming back at full force.

After returning to North Carolina, I believed things were picking up for us. I wanted to know where I stood with him. I questioned Michael if this 'dating thing' we had going on was essentially going somewhere. Are we in a relationship or were we free to see other people? Did he feel that I tried to rush him into a commitment or if I should have waited to see where it was going? He said that he wasn't dating anyone, but I doubt that he spoke the truth. How would I know since I didn't have communications with his family or friends? Now, I don't believe I rushed anything because of how he reacted to my questions. Shortly after I returned home, we experienced a terrible disagreement. I tried to call him to resolve our issues, but he was unresponsive. There were things I didn't know about Michael. Too much time passed and his actions and mood swings showed me the "new" him. We were out of contact for several years. It was of importance for me to know how many women he dated previously, his HIV status and if he was living on the 'down low.' Perhaps, he wasn't ready to comprehend the woman I grew up to be in his absence. He remembered the young naïve girl that fell in love with him. That girl was shy and reserved. Although my demeanor is conservative, I am far from irrational or irresponsible. Just because a person maybe single and available, it doesn't mean they are needy and accept all actions of a man. Life is too short and settling was just not an option.

LIFE LESSONS:

Although you've known someone for many, many years that doesn't mean that they're the same person today. It's wonderful to reminisce on memories but take that person at face value. Listen closely to what they're saying to you. Often, you can tell if there is drama and deep tribulations shown and heard through their behaviors and speech. Sometimes counseling is necessary but it's hard getting an African-American man to convey his personal business.

Michael shocked me by his defiant stand on not expressing his views openly. When he stopped calling, it clearly upset and surprised me. His attitude bothered me. It's obvious that he was upset because of our disagreement. I honestly thought that we could resolve it, but Allah had another plan for us. There aren't any guarantees when it comes to getting to know someone and what they're thinking.

    Men, in general, totally think different from women. When you're upfront at the beginning of the relationship, somehow, they tend not to tell the entire truth. Sometimes the truth isn't revealed until you're face-to-face with their wives or girlfriends. They will slip up and say the wrong thing at the wrong time. It's a cat and mouse chase, but at a mature age, things should change. History has shown me that age is nothing but a number. Take every situation individually. Not all men have drama and become unfaithful to their significant other. However, on the other hand, some people never change.

"No man can do anything to you that you do not allow him to do. He will not change for you. He will not conform to your dreams of what a real man is in your eyes. It is what it is. Do not conceal facts. Truth hurts."

(Yasmeen Abdur-Rahman)

Chapter 10: Love Is Blind: Get Your Third Eye Examined

Have you ever heard the phrase about a person having an "old soul?" Well, that description fit Jalil to a tee. When Jalil and I met, we were young. He was 15 years old and I was 18 years old. I didn't think that he was as young as he was, because of the way he carried himself. The first time we laid eyes on one another, the chemistry was unthinkable. It was love at first sight; well, change that . . . it was lust at first sight. I will be the first to admit that his style of love blinded my judgments. He was a breath of fresh air. Jalil was not anything like any of the men I dated in the past.

He dated women who were at least five years his senior, and that no doubt added to his irresistible swagger. Jalil was a smooth operator who knew how to whisper all the right things in my ears. His game was tight! He wasn't the typical youngster growing up in Jersey! He read books on how to pleasure a woman. He knew how to treat my body in the way that every woman desires. He came up with ideas that my brain would never think of, and his exploratory thoughts kept the magic alive behind closed doors. When he said, 'I love you,' it felt as if I was the only woman in his world. That was far from the truth!

When we first met, Jalil juggled several women and his main girlfriend became pregnant with his first daughter. We were not in an exclusive relationship. There were times when all of us would end up in the same nightclub. I admit that it felt painful seeing him exchange conversations with other women, but he ended up at my house by the end of the night. At the time, I called him my 'jump off.' Later when I went through a devastating separation from my husband (more on that later), I knew I could call on him. He's the "Maintenance Man' who supplied me with affection and intimacy that my husband was lavishing on other women. The mother of Jalil's daughter lived in the South. He took bi-weekly trips down South to be with them. With the women in his life, he told many lies to be at more than one place at a time. He became a professional liar. It sometimes felt like I had loved Jalil forever. After all, our friendship spans over 30 years. During most of that time, except the 10 years of my marriage to my ex-husband, we experienced an on again/off again relationship. That is a whole lot of years and a whole lot of memories.

Jalil was a sharp dresser which was one of the things that initially caught my eye. Instead of wearing jogging suits and sneakers, like most boys and men in the neighborhood, he wore custom-made, tailored suits and stylish, expensive shoes along with diamond jewelry. I wondered if he owned a pair of sneakers. He wore expensive diamond watches and rings and drove a red Mercedes Benz and Cadillac. Jalil amazed me with his maturity and confidence in relationships and life in general. Jalil's street mentality kept him attentive. He became the ultimate street hustler! If he were to write a book, it would be on the bestseller's list.

The knowledge he gained from running the streets probably paved the way for the person he is today – the good and bad side of him. The entire time I have known Jalil, he never mentioned his dad at all. When his mother served her sentence in prison for selling drugs, he became the adult of his family. Selling drugs came natural to him because he took on adult responsibilities at a young age.

His personal mission was to make sure his family was taken care of financially in the event something happened to him – be it a premature death or a prison sentence. I guess you could say that there was a method to the madness. There I stood, young and naïve, caught up in his lifestyle.

Regrettably, the street lifestyle ended abruptly in 1995. Jalil was sentenced to prison for ten years for robbing banks, amongst other illegal transactions. My friends called to see if I recognized him on the news. It shocked me and felt surreal. By the time this transpired, my divorce was concluding and we were in one of our "on again" phases.

The situation felt strange that I did not hear from Jalil for about a year after he went to prison. To say that it pissed me off would be an understatement. Secretly in my mind the relationship was a done deal. One day out of the blue, he called me (collect of course) as if nothing was wrong between us. I was still 'his girl.'

I can't describe the hold that he had on me. For seven of the ten years that he was incarcerated, we maintained an on again/off again relationship. Regularly, I found time to visit with Jalil at several of his prison locations. A part of me could not believe that I was willingly walking into a prison to visit someone. This was a new experience for me because in the past, when my uncles or family members went to prison, visiting them was never an option.

The visitations were extremely uncomfortable. There were instructions to take off your coat and no personal belongings were permitted on the premises. You could bring in money for the vending machines and your identification and that was it. Some Muslim women were fully covered. Some women were barely wearing anything at all; they looked like prostitutes. It shocked me to see inmates having sex with their visitor's right in front of the correction officers. At one point, while covered as a Muslim, it was awkward because a female guard directed me to the ladies' room to search my scarf for weapons and contraband. Depending on where he was located, I stood out in the crowd in my Islamic attire.

We discussed marriage all the time with full details to match. He requested me to send him pictures of engagement rings so that he had an idea of what to purchase for me. I found out later that he purchased engagement rings for almost every woman that he dated. A true playa to the end!

I was crazy in love with Jalil. I couldn't see how he was manipulating me. My heart melted each time he called for me. After receiving a letter in the mail, I went to a quiet space in my apartment to read it word for word repeatedly. It highlighted one of the good parts of my day. He stated that he loved me repetitively. My phone bills were exceedingly high because accepting collect calls from prison was preposterous but I made sure it was paid to avoid missing his calls. Could you imagine how much money that was spent on stamps because we wrote each other so much that our letters crossed in the mail?

Loving Jalil was like a habit; the habit I just couldn't kick. I inherited an unsaid nickname throughout our relationship. His friends in prison and from our neighborhood knew me as 'The Good Sister.' Ironically, they all knew that I would never bring drama to Jalil's lifestyle. I was shy and modest. Since most of his friends are Muslims, they loved to see us together. I covered my hair and they admired that in me. Many of his friends that are Muslims wanted their wives to wear the Islamic attire but they refused. I never argued with Jalil. I never made waves with his girlfriends or women that he knew in his past. It felt funny hearing him call his friends and say – Oh; 'the good sister' is on the phone or sitting next to me. There were so many 'hidden' agenda's with Jalil and I was one of them. You could see from the huge smile on his face, that he was happy about me being in his life.

Lastly, after ten years of incarceration, Jalil made it to the halfway house. Some inmates had the opportunity to live in a transitional home to prepare them for society living. This is a place where you find a job before your official release from prison. During his first transition, I took a train ride from North Carolina to Jersey to see him. It felt good, but also strange to be in a room with Jalil without guards, cameras or bob-wired fencing. I was still on edge even though there wasn't anyone watching. I honestly thought that we would finally get an opportunity to live as a couple after his transitional period. Unfortunately, Jalil's return to civilian life was short-lived. You see, when the authorities allow you an early release, you are heavily scrutinized and closely watched. Any minor infraction or something as simple as an anonymous phone call will increase your chances of returning to prison to complete your original sentence. That's exactly what happened to Jalil. His daughter's Mother called the authorities with accusations about him. He returned to prison. When he called me on the telephone with the terrible news, he was upset and I, too, was upset and confused. This meant my dreams of us being a family went on hold once again, but that didn't stop our relationship. When he went back to prison, we continued to burn the phone lines and postal service up with our communications. In my head, my relationship with Jalil was great and it would only be a matter of time before he was released from prison and we became husband and wife.

    Unfortunately, Jalil failed to tell me that he rekindled a relationship with a woman from his past. He claimed that I knew they were still communicating on the phone. Yes, he told me that they were friends. The way that I found out about his transgression was in a casual telephone conversation with his sister. She assumed I was okay with Jalil seeing the two of us at the same time. Since his sister was aware of the religious observant that Jalil and I practiced, it wouldn't have been a surprise to her at all, if I agreed to that arrangement. Nevertheless, that wasn't the case at all. Jalil was not married to either of us. He wasn't practicing Islam to the letter. At first, I thought, we are both Muslims. Why not handle this as such and approach the arrangements in the open? Honestly, at the time, I would have considered a polygyny arrangement. In the Islamic religion, a man could have up to four wives at a time; it is not considered cheating in Islam. Although, in the USA only one wife is legal, it meant that he could create other homes with other women according to the religious guidelines. The real problem was that this woman wasn't accepting this religious setup. She is not a Muslim. It's inconceivable how much she did not know about Jalil that I had full access to my entire life. What was so heartbreaking is that he decided to cheat on me after all that we had gone through. Out of the love that we found for one another, how could he treat me this way? I was furious with him and could not wait to get his telephone call that night.

    Of course, once we communicated, he talked to me as if I was imagining everything. Lying was second nature to him. He should have told me the truth. The truth of the matter is Jalil secured himself a place to live after his release from prison. He started dating this woman and making promises to her because she provided a place to stay in Jersey, a car, a job and connections for his release. He needed an address to use and someone to help him rebuild his credit. Everything fell in place for him. Since we were not legally married, he could not relocate to North Carolina to be with me. Inmates are released in the state where the crimes took place as a part of parole requirements. Therefore, she looked more and more enticing to Jalil by the moment. This woman had no clue that he and I planned to be together, or did she? She knew that we were involved in the past but thought it was over. Jalil told her that I began to date an ex-boyfriend from my past. I'm sure she was comfortable after hearing that lie. In her eyes, there wasn't a threat to their newfound relationship. Jalil made sure she did not marry anyone, have children, or get involved seriously with other men while he was incarcerated. He yearned for more children and she could provide that for him. Jalil was well aware that I could not give him any children. I was no longer of interest to him on a financial or emotional level.

This relationship made me feel like an inmate because I placed countless restrictions on myself and took on that lifestyle. At the beginning, only my closest friends and a few of my relatives knew about my relationship with Jalil. Jalil told everyone in his family, especially his uncles about us. My girlfriends thought that it was foolish to think that something great would come from this type of connection. Why was I wasting so much time on this man? For five years straight, I did not date anyone. I became celibate. I moved in my day-to-day world as a woman in a relationship, and never thought about cheating on him or moving forward without Jalil. Jalil made me feel as if I was his wife and I owed him faithfulness. My friends tried to 'hook me up' with people but I declined with excuses. Of course, many men from my past could have taken my mind off Jalil. The web of lies and deceit had me unstable all the time. Jalil became the first thought in my day. It was astounding how his existence allowed him to take me away from family, friends and business projects that required my full attention. I knew that some men in jail behaved in this way, but not Jalil. I had a history with him, so I did not feel like the scorned pen pal. My allegiance to Jalil was steadfast and eternal. Everything he said to me felt like the truth because of his unconditional love. Why would he want to hurt me?

Jalil constantly said that he would never get married to anyone other than me. He never told the truth, so it did not shock me when I got the news of his marriage. Jalil told me that she desired to get married before their daughter was born. Around my birthday in May 2006, he started acting strange. If she knew her husband and his devious, cheating ways, she would be shocked.

However, he had always been that way. Perhaps her head is in the clouds? His motto is – a man can do what he wants to do because he's a man. Part of this theory comes from the streets and the other part comes from the older men he hung out with growing up. If that was the way men in his life treated women, it was only natural that he would mimic their behaviors. He did not grow up with his dad explaining to him how to treat women with respect and honesty. This is a sad state of affairs because many African-American men lack self-control and commitment. Just like my ex-husband, Jalil did not have a clue.

His wife sat home dreaming about creating a family with a man who lived for a pimp award. Marriage did not stop him from cheating. In my mind, I knew I should not open my door or accept his phone calls, but he was my addiction. When he called and I did not answer, he got upset. He sat in front of my apartment and called me from his cell phone. He tried to see if another man visited me. He called me every morning while on his way to work. He called after work. When I wasn't available for him, he began to argue and ask why I would not pick up my cell phone or was not home when he came by to visit me. It was almost as if he was my husband. He said his wife wouldn't leave him regardless if she found out about me or any other women in his life. That may be true because she was brainwashed. He created that falsehood for me as well. He told me not to tell people about us, especially my friends who knew her too. Someone once asked me this question – "How does it feel to be the love of his life in secret?" It is crazy! We seldom went anywhere together to avoid being seen in public. My apartment was his safe-haven. When he was there, he played the role of the man of the house. My apartment, in his eyes, was his other residence. He went in the refrigerator for food and asked me what was for dinner the next night. When I moved in my new place, his first question was – Where is my key? He called me to hear what I wore to bed that night. He deceived his wife every time he called me, when he gave me money, when he thought about me, and when he made love to me. It felt unfair to me when we were together. It's easier for a man to love more than one woman without blinking an eye. When women love, we love hard. Men appear to be able to conceal their emotions and store them away when it suits the situation.

I finally came to the decision to end the unhealthy relationship. The reality was that Jalil would never be the man for me. He continued to lie and cheat to keep his marriage sacred. He called me from the home he shared with his wife. He was predictable. He was not worthy of my love and affection. This was a huge adjustment for me. Sleeping around with him became habitual and comfortable. You can get content with a situation even if it's not the right one for you. Outside of the sex, we had little in common. It felt good while it lasted. I dreamed of him changing. Most women have that dream too but they would not admit to it. He said what I wanted to hear, and I accepted all of it. I believed no matter what happened, everything would remain the same with us. Jalil was convinced that single or married, I would be a part of his life. I refused to accept that! Ironically, when I told Jalil that I was looking for a husband, he immediately began to call me every derogatory name in the dictionary. His pride was hurt and bruised. He wanted to hurt me. I laughed hysterically because this man was married. The only thing that resonated in his mind was another man was going to be sleeping with me. It came back to the sex issue. I told him to go to his wife and admit his infidelities and start over again, but I realized who I was talking to and started to laugh again.

In the end, finally, Jalil spoke the truth. We were having a conversation and he said to me, "Nothing that I say will change anything." Now, that was a light bulb moment. It felt as if time stood still. Finally, for the first time, he spoke the truth!

My common sense left my body when it came to Jalil. I forgot everything that I knew to be the truth just to feel a moment of happiness. I blocked so many blessings by putting myself in situations like this one. I prayed every day that I grow strong enough to move forward to find the man that can give me all that I deserve. Struggling not to be alone or used like most of the women in my family – another generation of lonely women. Why did I gravitate to the same type of men? I knew wrong from right. I considered myself a reasonably, smart woman. My heart deters me the wrong way. Perhaps, it was GOD's decree for me to go through these lessons. I wondered if I allowed myself to be with these men, because I wanted someone to take the place of my dad. The older women in my family said that you marry men who tend to have characteristics of your dad.

While incarcerated, he became in-depth with Islam and discovered how to become a better person. Was it just jail talk? He is a seasoned criminal. In 2010, Jalil was incarcerated again! He just couldn't get out of the system.

LIFE LESSONS:

Trust is something that I experienced little of in my past relationships. All of them ended in deceit. The lessons I grasped are priceless. No amount of money could fulfill the emptiness that I have suffered. You think you know a man by the length of time you're around him, by the commitment of their voice, and by the financial and emotional bonds. I guess you could say that I am a hopeless romantic.

While growing up, I searched to find the 'right' man. In Islam, it's not permissible to date. Encounters are with the person you're interested in marrying along with your Wali (guardian); you're never alone with them at all, until marriage.

They say that men who are close with their mothers are a great catch. My ex-boyfriends and ex-husband all have close relationships with their mothers. I found it puzzling at times and perhaps that is a myth. Even though I find that to be somewhat true, there are still issues that some men have with their dad's absences or lack of support. Unfortunately, each of my relationships were similar yet different.

Never allow a man to take 'control' over your life. Once he realizes that you're emotionally hooked, he will begin to pick apart your spirit and soul. You will begin to fit into his standards. If a man who won't be honest with you about his past and present life approaches you, run for the hills. He will lie to you. One lie leads to another lie.

If you're dating an incarcerated man, think twice about how it may end upon his release. He may get out of prison and feel his way back to running the streets and seeing other women. If he was a cheater on the streets, trust that your chances of being cheated on is 100 percent. Plus, most of them continue to run game and live illegal lives in jail. If he has spent a substantial amount of time locked up, stay woke!

"It's easier to ask forgiveness than it is to get permission."
(Grace Hopper)

"Once a woman has forgiven her man, she must not reheat his sins for breakfast."
(Marlene Dietrich)

"Too often the strong, silent man is silent only because he does not know what to say and is reputed strong only because he has remained silent."
(Sir Winston Churchill)

Chapter 11: Until Death or the Other Woman Do Us Part

Raymond came into my life unexpectedly. At the time, I was 20 years old and grasping how vulnerable it was to be in a relationship. Meeting someone was far from my mind. My cousin Shelly insisted that I meet with Raymond. Undeniably, she said that this man was for me. She was persistent on the issue. You see, they met first. Shelly didn't think he was her type. They became platonic friends. I finally agreed to meet Raymond so she would stop bugging me.

One night, she came to my house for me to style her hair. Afterwards, she invited Raymond to come by and the rest is history. My first impression of Raymond was that he was tall and handsome. He seemed polite and mature. Shortly after our first meeting, we began to talk to each other on the telephone every day. Raymond worked nights. I worked days. This made it harder to find quality time to spend together. Whenever we did find time for a date, it was phenomenal. Something as simple as sitting in front of the television sharing a bowl of popcorn or dining in the secluded part of a restaurant were special moments. We were both surprised that we connected on all levels so fast. Our bond was solid. We fell in love at high speed. We didn't see it coming.

A few months after we met, we began to date exclusively. At least that's what I thought. Guess what? Raymond already had a girlfriend. One woman wasn't enough for him. One day, while driving down High Street in Newark, his "girlfriend" spotted me from her seat on the bus. Apparently, she lived on High Street, and everyone knew his black Nissan Maxima. Raymond was cocky. He encouraged me to drive right past his girlfriend's house. Did Raymond want to get caught? He never detoured me in another driving direction.

Raymond and I reached his home that he shared with his Mom in Union. The girlfriend was sitting in the living room talking to his mother. She was crying and trying to figure out why he was cheating on her. I was speechless. How did I get caught up in this drama? Of course, Raymond lied when he claimed to be single and available. That night, I found out from the girlfriend that they were recently on vacation together. She purchased Raymond gifts on her credit cards during their relationship. She was hurt. As another woman, I felt her pain. How could this go ignored? It was painfully obvious that Raymond was good at not telling the whole truth. That was a "red flag" but I was in love and blinded by his ability to sway the truth and speak my love language. When most women fall in love, we look the other way. Especially when it's obvious that we are being led down a road of heartache.

Within a year to the date we met, Raymond proposed marriage to me. At first, it was scary. We did not know each other well enough for an engagement. The incident with the girlfriend played in the back of my mind. However, I put my doubts aside and accepted his proposal. Yep, I said yes!

As I thought about what my parents would say, especially my dad, the tightness of my stomach felt like knots of rope twisted together. Although, I was grown and able to make my own decisions, my dad looked down on any man trying to get close to his little girl. I remember when I called my dad to break the news of our engagement to him. His first question to me was, "How well do you know this guy?" Since we wanted to get married as soon as possible, we agreed that having a smaller ceremony could help us save money. That money could be used to purchase a new car or put a down payment on a house. Planning a huge wedding would have required expert timing and a whole lot of money. We decided to go to the 'Justice of the Peace.' I went to Bamberger's (now known as Macy's) for a new dress. He purchased a new suit and pair of shoes. The ceremony was over in less than 10 minutes, with no fanfare. His parents, my mother, and other family members attended, but not my dad. My dad was extremely upset with me for accepting Raymond's marriage proposal. He intended for me to marry a Muslim man. Daddy never second-guessed his decisions. He boycotted the ceremony. We did not go on a honeymoon. Instead, Raymond's family prepared and surprised us with a wonderful backyard cookout.

After we were married, we moved in with Mother. Things

appeared to be going well the first month into our marriage. However, little things started happening to make me question my marriage to Raymond. It seemed like Raymond planned and attended events without his wife. We barely spent any quality time together. We spent more time with other people and less time together. Everyone we knew was single. Trying to find married couples to spend time with was obsolete. I guess you can say that we were both trying to get accustomed to being married. Do you remember the "red flag" moment with the girlfriend? Well, it turns out that my husband was a "playa" in the truest sense of the word. This had become a pattern of men that came into my life.

It didn't take him long to get back into action after we were married. We worked for the same pharmaceutical company. He cheated with women at the same company where we worked. My husband had no limitations to places that he found women to cheat on me with. I recall sitting at my desk at work hearing fellow co-workers gossip in the hallway about my husband. It was an embarrassing and painful feeling. My marriage should have been dissolved immediately. There were times when women called my house at three in the morning. When I answered, they would hang up. He drove them around in my brand-new car. He lied about losing his wedding band. Later, it was revealed that a woman threw it out of a moving car – my car. In the beginning, it felt like this would destroy our marriage. Raymond seemed sincere while making up for his discretions by promising not to cheat again. I did not file for a divorce because I was in love, comfortable and financially stable with Raymond. Staying with a man after infidelity was the route that most women endured back in those days.

For 10 years of marriage, Raymond cheated on me. He conceived a child with another woman (the same one who threw his wedding ring out of my car as she was riding in it)! Finding out that he impregnated another woman was traumatic. I remember vividly the day I came home to hear the bad news that he fathered a daughter! We were both sitting on the bed. I was at the foot of the bed putting on my shoes. In my mind, I thought he said he had an older daughter that wasn't disclosed to me. Sadly, that was not the case. When he told me the dreadful news, I picked up the remote and threw it at him out of anger. He tried to console me but the only thing I wanted to do was get away from him. When this woman was pregnant, his mother and sister attended her baby shower. My in-laws purchased an expensive crib for his daughter. Later they purchase the exact same crib when my son was born. Sometimes when I think back about this situation, it annoys me. My in-laws deceived my trust, too. They were my family. They took on my husband's infidelity as if I didn't matter. If anyone should have told me about my husband, it should have been his mother. She knew all about his character and his history with women. She protected and lied for him. One thing I will not do for my son is protect him from his deceit. After going through so much pain, I would not allow him to put me in his lies or give him permission to deceive women in my presence. My life would have turned out differently if honesty was at the beginning of my relationship. My mental spirit and my heart were broken into miniature pieces. Mother was the only person who knew about my marital chaos. It was humiliating once the 'cat was out of the bag.' Everyone looked up to our picture-perfect marriage. In the eyes of most, he did no wrong. That was a stressful time in my life. Living day to day with the whole situation was complicated.

Shortly after finding out that Raymond had fathered a daughter, my pregnancy test was positive! My pregnancy went well and without complications until the car accident that happened during my sixth month. A man driving down a block to buy drugs in Newark drove through a stop sign and hit my car. I am thankful to Allah that my seatbelt remained fastened because my son may not have lived to see the light of day. Someone who witnessed the accident called 911 for help. After a week of hospitalization and careful observations of my pregnancy, it turned out that my baby and I were healthy. Just when it appeared Raymond calmed down with his infidelities, he instead continued to spiral out of control.

While in bed restraints after the car accident, my husband called to say that he was on his way to visit me in the hospital so I patiently waited for him to arrive. Since I was eager to see him, I struggled out of the hospital bed to look out the window for his arrival. As soon as I reached the window, a girl driving his car dropped him off at the front of the hospital door. It was as if all my husband's lies fell in my lap! It amazed me that my son was born healthy and without complications due to the stress that I was under my entire pregnancy.

On a hot summer day, on July 12, 1989, Raymond Jr. was born. Raymond Jr was 21 inches long, 7 pounds and 12 ounces in size. His head covered completely with long, jet black curly hair. Our baby boy was a replica of my baby pictures. I came home with a breathtaking, bundle of joy. Of course, all parents believe that their baby is the most captivating baby in the world. I could not believe this little baby was mine. He was perfect.

In the hospital, the mother instinct in me wanted to breast-feed him. We did not bond at all and that made me sad. Postpartum Depression took over my emotions and state of mind. When holding my son, he cried uncontrollably. It felt like we were strangers. I believe that my son felt my emotional detachment from him. Thankfully, we were still living with Mother. Mother helped with her brand-new grandson.

He was a quiet baby and observant. The only time he cried was when it was time to give him a bath. My husband connected instantly with Raymond Jr and our son adored him. When Raymond Jr heard his father's voice, he became mesmerized. Raymond changed our son's diapers and placed him on his chest as he fell asleep. You can say he spoiled him rotten. Raymond Jr was at peace around his father. It was such a precious moment to see them connect. My experience with the two of them together was priceless. During this time, pictures were being snapped left and right. Every day after work, Raymond came home to bathe and clothe our son before "going out for air." Majority of the time, he took our baby with him on his outdoor adventures. He showed him off to his friends and relatives.

A few months after our baby was born, we were financially ready to move out of my mother's home. We moved to an apartment in Jersey where Raymond Sr grew up. Everyone knew my husband. His family lived in a small tight-knit community. The area was safe. It was helpful that his family lived nearby.

Union was a suburban neighborhood compared to other local areas of Jersey. Unlike Newark, Union had tall trees surrounded by grassy, manicured lawns. The streets were clean. The area was layered with single-family homes managed by proud homeowners. This was a great place to raise our son. Normally, it would have been expensive to live in Union. We were fortunate to know the property owner of a four-family house. Raymond Sr attended college with her grandson. She kindly offered us a lower rental rate and we were grateful.

Of course, Raymond Sr was still sneaking around but I continued to stay. Raymond worked hard, took care of his family, and made sure that we materially had everything possible. This was probably his way of feeling better after each affair. In the end, he figured that no one could say that he did not take care of his family. That is the mindset of a cheating husband.

My marriage continued to keep my son happy. Since I grew up without my dad in our household, I did not want my son to endure his father's absence. Something had to give in our marriage so we decided to separate. After my husband left, my son and I missed him and yearned for him to return home. It was my impression that while we were separated, we were trying to work on 'saving' our marriage. Apparently, Raymond had other ideas. Even though he told me that he wanted our family back together, he continued to cheat on me with other women. Women drove his car and he even entertained women at his mother's home. My son suffered the pain and anguish that I felt as a child after his father left. Everything fell apart.

After dropping by unannounced and seeing a woman in his bedroom, something finally clicked in my head. I call it my "light bulb" moment - again. It was time for me to move on. Therefore, in 1994, after 10 years of happiness, chaos and sadness, I finally got up the courage to file for a divorce. My son was 4 years old. The exact same age when my parents separated. The divorce decree was quickly typed and signed. When filing for an uncontested divorce, it wasn't necessary for Raymond to be present when our case went before the judge. Our marriage dissolved in less than 5 minutes. Ironically almost the same amount of time that it took a judge to marry us ten years earlier. Raymond called me. He did not believe me when I told him I was filing for a divorce. When I called him at work to give the news that we were officially and legally divorced, he thought it was a joke. When he came by and saw the copy of the divorce decree, his mouth dropped to the floor. Our marriage was over.

LIFE LESSONS:

What I know to be a fact is that my ex-husband wasn't going to divorce me. He was happy with being able to stop by to visit when he felt the need to show his face. He did not want to be judged on being divorced. He wanted to keep his 'nice guy' persona. Divorce was never ever spoken out of his mouth.

In the end, my life exposed me to men who weren't faithful or committed to our relationships. Without these experiences, I would not know what it takes to be a friend, mother, girlfriend or a wife.

In addition, these situations have shown me what types of men are available and how they treat women. Experiences are your best teacher. If you do not grasp lessons from them, you are doomed to repeat them. Some mistakes can be costly. Some will cost you mental anguish and a life of uncertainties. Others can be minute crossroads throughout your travels. My prayers were that my future husband is a man ready to embark on a good relationship with an ambitious woman who is moving forward with grace.

My son is now an adult. He took on some of the characteristics of both his parents, good and bad. He is a ladies' man. He produced a baby out of wedlock. I prayed that as he got older, he would mature and act accordingly. It's not too late.

"Raising a child alone is one of the hardest jobs in my life. If you don't have any children, you will never understand how powerful that statement is for me."

(Yasmeen Abdur-Rahman)

Chapter 12: A Fatherless Child

While going through my high school years, I specifically remember saying to my friends that marriage and having children was out of the question. The fear of desertion was the main reason why my thoughts were this way. In my immature mind, my dad left me. After a devastating divorce, I found myself as a single parent, just like Mother. This was a road that I never planned to drive down, ever. Destiny stepped in and my life altered forever.

My perception of a family portrait is a husband, wife and one child or children. The divorce destroyed our family structure. My heart broke into millions of pieces with every lie that he told during our marriage. Like most women, I picked up the pieces and pushed forward. When we met, I meticulously expressed my concerns with having children and raising them alone. Knowing how my ex-husband's father disappointed him, I thought that Raymond's priorities were to be a strong entity in our sons' life. It wasn't about the money because it takes more than a check to raise a child. Most fathers do not have a clue as to why the money is never enough to raise a child in these disconcerting times.

From time to time, I wondered how I was not walking around talking to myself like a mentally insane person. Every now and then, it felt like I was having a nervous breakdown. How did I function in this untamed, unfair world?

At first, I managed to make ends meet financially due to limitless job opportunities after the divorce. Job stability kept the lights on and the rent paid every month. Money isn't the single most significant element of maintaining as a single parent. After the divorce, my ex-husband emotionally disconnected from our son's every day needs. It became my purpose as his mother to become the go-to person in my son's life. Being "Super Mommy" took its toll on my life. Emotionally, it made me exhausted. There weren't many people to lean on for support besides Mother and a few close friends. My life escalated downhill. My job was to be strong for my son and that was challenging. My son has seen me at my lowest moments. Crying in front of him when he could not understand where my pain came from put me in a dark place in my life. It was difficult to stand tall every day. It looked as if everything was in order. The truth was that everything was out of order. When everything looks wonderful from the outside and you feel like your world is crumbling from your inside, it's harder to fake it.

When I was unemployed, my son had a rude awakening and a different outlook on my position in our household. Our lifestyle changed radically. Purchasing extravagant food items from the grocery store or clothes shopping at any given time stopped instantaneously. In the past, we dined out frequently and never stressed about how we would get by. Money was spent as if there was no budget. That was an awesome feeling. While working at Novartis, each week my money went directly in my checking account. Even though he felt the difference, my son still did not have a clue when the rent was due or if I could cover next month's rent. Children are so innocent. Signing up with several temporary agencies to keep money flowing in while seeking a permanent position was critical. That situation constantly kept me on the edge while creating opportunities by way of my home-based business. If a contract assignment passed me by, we could have easily become homeless. Some people say that, jokingly, but that was my reality. At first, keeping in contact with business clients and applying my knowledge to new services helped tremendously. Being able to work from home, setup my own hours and fees was great. It was what I dreamed of but not under those circumstances. At that time, my plan B was working for me. This situation brought on an ideal boost of self-confidence.

Unfortunately, when business was slow, my frustrations and anxieties came back rapidly. When my friends found out how dismal my situation was, they were upset with me. I held back my pain and discord without seeking support from them. My closest friends stepped in to give me assistance monetarily and emotionally. Mother raised an independent person. It was difficult to allow my friends to know of my hardship.

At best, child support kept food on the table. It felt great knowing that there was not a fight to get it. Now I realize that I should have sought after increases. The projection for a baby is different to what's necessary for a teenager who is 6'5 in height, a size 15-shoe at 220 pounds. Just like Mother, the same pattern of not going to court for support brought on unnecessary anguish. One day, the light bulb moment happened again. My ex-husband was mandated by the courts to pay child support. He shopped for our son at least 4 times a year. He purchased whatever our son wished for at the drop of a hat. I remember one day, my ex-husband and I argued about how the child support money was spent. It offended me to my core to explain to Raymond how the child support was being spent on our son! If my light bill is due, the money went to that bill. If my rent was due and the money was accessible, it went towards my rent for that month. It shocked me that my ex-husband treated me like some 'chicken head' from the projects. Chicken head was an inner-city slang used for young mothers with lots of children and baby fathers. I was not lazy or fighting an addiction. When our son lived with him for a short timeframe, he realized how the money does not cover his living expenses. When he purchased food every week, he thought twice about questioning my abilities as a parent. He hated to admit that he was wrong with his allegations. Men should be educated on what it takes to raise a child, especially for a single parent alone. They have this ridiculous perception that women take their money to harm them, when, in fact, the children are the reason why they are sending the money in the first place. If they get past the fact that the ex-wife or girlfriend is sleeping with someone else, remarried or if she is driving a new car, everything would run smoothly. That mindset goes both ways; for the father raising their children without the mother as well.

    Operating as a single parent was a constant worry for me all the time. Raymond Jr seemed determined to 'show out' in school instead of using this venue as a learning tool towards his future. He went to school lacking classroom participation, not completing homework or daily school projects. He attended a private, religious school, but never focused on his schooling or religious studies. Attending a Muslim school was not free or subsidized. He was transferred back to public schools. His teachers commented that he was an intelligent young man. They were amazed how he passed statewide tests but did not apply himself in a classroom setting. When he was willing to comprehend the materials taught, it would shed light to his personality in school. Unfortunately, at the time, he was so immature that everything to him was a joke. There weren't any programs or vouchers accessible for me. I was not on welfare. When we moved to North Carolina, he was demoted a year because of his grades and attendance. Throughout numerous, lengthy speeches about education, I told him those dreadful grades would sneak up on him one day.

When we relocated to North Carolina, my ex-husband rarely called my son. In most cases, I left messages on his voicemail. We never received responses from him unless it was an emergency. My son managed to get major attention from his father when he was younger. When Raymond, Jr became a young adult, his father rarely came around at all. The visits to North Carolina started to become non-existent. Sometimes I wondered why he was not willing to take a week off from both of his jobs to spend quality time with him. Are his jobs that important? Not being able to spend time with his father took a toll on my son. We sought counseling as he began to act out in school. My son needed to talk to someone who he could trust without picking sides. It was obvious that he missed his father profoundly. When my ex-husband remarried, Raymond Jr experienced yet another drastic change. His father spent time with his daughter, the one he conceived during our marriage, but failed to see that our son was calling out for help.

My son is tall, dark and handsome. He's affectionate. He makes you want to yell, stop, please. He's passionate about knowing if I love him or not. He says, 'I love you' every other hour in a single day. He's attentive. Ultimately, it's all about making the right choices. Sometimes I wondered if his personality stems from our divorce – the disappointment of desertion. Surely, I understood what he was feeling. One thing that concerned me was the disrespectfulness. As much as we have gone through together, he saddened me in one of the worse ways a child could to their parents. Immediately after I stopped spanking him, he began to talk back. I never talked back to my parents. I know that they did not raise me to be disrespectful to anyone. I knew that my parents worked their butts off for me to have something fashionable to wear to school. My parents were strict. We were popped in the mouth if anything was said sarcastically. My son thought because of his height that in some way he had authority over me. These days, kids are not fearful of their parents! They take many risks when it comes to what they say and do. I feared that Raymond Jr wouldn't recognize my support was unconditional. No other support jumped to help me with anything outside of my mother. Anytime he needed help, he called me first; not his father. Yet, he disrespected me with his mouth.

If a male role model lived with us, things could have turned out differently. A woman can't give a boy the true insight as to how to become a man. Many African-American men are in dreadful relationships, incarcerated, or dealing with abusive situations. They have had a hard time with commitments and trust stemming from the way their Mothers raised them. Not to say that Mothers are totally at fault because men have a mind of their own and know wrong from right. As Mothers, we tend to pamper our sons to the point that they expect their future wife to cater to them on all levels. When there is one child involved, it's obvious that you tend to spread the love thick and overlook some of the shortcomings that they may experience.

In September of 2006, my son started to understand why I preached to him about life. He began working two jobs and seemed eager to reach his goals. He took out the garbage, became respectable to me, and we were getting along well. This change made me feel happy and proud to be his mother. We came a long way but unfortunately, this newfound image did not last long.

In 2007, my son announced to me that he joined the gang. I felt devastated, sad, irate, mortified and petrified for him and myself. He asked, 'What would you do if I were in a gang?' My response was, 'Kick you out of my house.' In the next second, I realized he was on his way to make the statement that parents never wanted to hear from their child's mouth. My son told me that he joined the gang two years ago. As we sat at the kitchen table, it felt like this was all a dream. Ironically, the day before his announcement I shared with him several incidents in Jersey dealing with gang violence. My first reaction was anger. There were many thoughts running through my mind. It felt like I was hyperventilating. My stomach began to bubble up and the direction of the bathroom was my only concern. He followed me and we embraced. Then after settling down, he continued telling me his story. When I asked why he wanted to join a gang, his answer turned out to be a conversation that I will never forget. He started by saying that his return to Jersey set everything into motion. His relationship with his father went from happiness to horrible. His father shocked him when there was not a suitable place for him to sleep other than the couch in his girlfriend's living room. The apartment was half the size of our apartment in North Carolina; at least he had his own bedroom. His father promised him that they were going to spend time together and each time nothing came out of it. His father promised him that he would get an apartment for them to share. Instead, our son watched him make his girlfriend's children a priority. One of the little girls even called his father, "Daddy." My son said he felt so alone. He wanted a father who played basketball with him, who took long rides with him, talked about life and let him know that everything would be okay. Instead, his father continued to make promises that he never intended to keep. He continued to give money to replace the time he should have spent with our son. His father was the one role model that he cherished and adored but the rejection pushed him to this decision of joining the gang.

During this long talk, I began to cry uncontrollably. I prayed he would avoid this lifestyle. It was inevitable for him to follow this route since he had a considerable amount of alone time on his hands. He was left unsupervised every day while living with his father.

From anger, my emotions went to guilt. I felt guilty because I did not recognize the warning signs. I noticed from time to time that he started to wear one color every day. The history of gangs was not something that I bookmarked on my computer. When he was younger, I knew his friend's parents. He interacted with the same kids from the neighborhood. Now, he wasn't focusing in school and his friendship base changed drastically. He stayed out late at night with his friends. Then one day I noticed that one of my kitchen knives was missing. Was he falling that low and put his family at risk but more importantly his own life? I tried to spend quality time with my son. He declined my invitations to the movies, dinner and other outside activities – another red flag. I distinguished all along that his father was the parent that he was eager to spend quality time with but I tried to keep him happy in my own way. This is what Mother's do for their children. We try to be all and do all when the father is not playing his part. I went from feeling guilty to feeling ashamed and embarrassed. I did not talk about this with Mother, other family members or friends. You hear about gang members on television. You hear about all the devastation they cause and now I was a parent who had one living in my home. I thought, what would people think of me? Will they think that I caused him to join a gang? Will they criticize me knowing that I have been in my son's corner all his life? It's easier for people to pass judgment on my character as a Mother knowing that they could be in the same predicament. I should not feel guilty at all. I know how society places the blame on the parents. My son never lived in a household that never cared about him or his well-being. I thought that I hovered over him too much. I thought that if I kept up with the music, sports and the activities that he liked, we would have more in common.

My son cried like a baby as he told his story. I was stunned to hear what was coming out of his mouth. He sold marijuana (weed), too! While living in Jersey, other gang members from opposite turfs chased him with guns from school. He feared for his life several times. The original story that he told me months earlier about people chasing him while walking to school was to some extent true. He failed to say they were rival gang members. As he sat there, what should I have done next? When I jokingly said that if I found out he was a gang member that I would throw him out my house, I could not imagine him walking the streets, eating out of garbage cans or stealing from another human being. I convinced myself that his lifestyle with this gang stuff would eventually end. I knew that I could not be with him every moment of the day. It was prayer that had me thinking that Raymond Jr would make better choices. Kids want to fit in. Like most gang members, he felt like the love at home was unbalanced. Children who have one ounce of hurt in their hearts or felt desertion by their fathers are likely to end up like my son. Please do not think that my story is rare. It is normal in the inner cities and suburbs. Most parents, just like me, do not have a clue that their children are gang members.

Although kicking him out of my house was an option, I decided to monitor him and his movements. The mother in me knew that he needed support and that is what I planned to do. Throughout our talk, the thought of calling his father rushed in my mind several times. In my mind, why tell him since he was one of the major reasons why this was happening? It's not as if he would take an emergency vacation from both his jobs and drive down to North Carolina for his son. Would our talk just turn into foul words? Right away, I felt he would blame me for everything. At first, my thoughts were not to tell him right away, but to allow my son to talk to him when he was ready. I left a message on his father's voicemail that we need to talk and he did not return my call. Instead, he called my son and asked him what I wanted. Raymond Jr never told him anything.

As my journey continued, I learned that my son had no strategies to get out of the gang. I took the initiative to contact a local detention program in the county where we resided. The information that I gathered from others is that most gang members are seeking a need that gangs meet for them. When they learn to meet their needs in a better way, they decide to stop being a gang member. However, for many gang members, the issue is not if they will grow out of being a gang member. The issue is whether they live long enough to make that decision. When gang members decide that they want to get out of the gang, there are steps that they can begin to follow. For one, you can never tell the gang you want out. You may be beaten or even killed. Begin spending your time doing other things. Instead of spending time with your gang friends, find something else to do during that time. Look around. There are possibilities everywhere: sports, recreation centers, Boys & Girl Clubs, arts programs, drama, school activities, and even spending time with family. Try to stop looking like a gangster. For many gang members, dressing down makes them feel safe because other people fear the way they look. As you begin to believe in yourself, you will find that you do not need to make other people feel afraid to feel good about yourself. Stop wearing the clothes that you think are gangster clothes. Stop talking like a gangster, acting like a gangster, and hanging out with gangsters. Find other things to say, other things to do, and other people to hang out with immediately. Get good at making excuses. Your parents can probably help you with this but if not, try asking a teacher or older friend for help. Some former gang members have said that when they started trying to get out, they stopped taking phone calls from their gang and had their family tell friends they weren't home. Find people that support you and believe in you. Getting out of gangs isn't a simple task but for sure, it's possible if you're serious about getting out of the gang. While sitting at work one day, my co-worker noticed that there was something wrong with me. After telling her that my son is out of control, she mentioned that her husband is a certified social worker and immediately a light went on in my head. After hearing what his job was and what affect he had on children, I decided to seek additional information for myself. Before the day was over at work, I emailed the organization with my situation. They offered help to children from seven to seventeen years old. My son was almost 18, at that time. If they could pick him up and place him in this program right away, it would save his life. If not, when my son turned 18 years old, we would have one last talk before changing my door locks and immediately removing him immediately from my lease. Who wants to live like a prisoner in their own home? Leaving my house unattended while my son was living with me was scary. There were times that I came home and both my front and back doors were unlocked. My safety kept me looking around as I stepped out of my car every day. He obviously did not care about himself, but I care about myself.

    If my son remained in Jersey, he would probably be dead right now. The way crime had escalated is horrible. Any parent should feel overwhelmed at keeping their children alive. Until I relocated back to Jersey, I did not believe that it was as bad as the news reports. Raising a son is one of the toughest jobs I have ever had that did not pay a salary.

In the end, one of my hardest decisions to make was to put my son out of my house. Ironically, it was time for me to renew my lease, but instead I sought after a new apartment in a completely new area of North Carolina. It was one of the saddest times of my life. It felt like I buried my son six feet under the ground. After a month or two of living alone, it became easier to manage and the guilt began to fade away.

Eventually, he moved back to Jersey with his father and with his grandmother, temporarily. He was accepted into a Job Corp program in Albany, NY but after several months, that did not work out either. I continued to pray for my son. It would take years for me to trust him again.

After living with Mother for months, she moved to a charming neighborhood in West Orange. He was notified that no one else was occupying her apartment. The last week of her moving process, he went to the nearest shelter. It hurt my heart that my son just did not get it. He went to jail for selling drugs again. He had me fooled to believe that he was going to make the right choices. The only advice that is open for him is to find Allah, obey Allah and ask Him for clarity. There is nothing else I can do for my son that I have not done already that has cost me my heart. I pray for him daily.

LIFE LESSONS:

My advice to all single parents is to maintain your sanity. Plan a monthly trip for yourself at a day spa, an overnight trip to an extravagant hotel with a jacuzzi tub, or a long walk on the beach. Allow your family and friends to support you as often as possible. Learn to say no when someone asks for your assistance, because I know, in the past, I have over-extended myself repeatedly.

Tell your children every day that you love them. Even if you two just had an intense argument, step away from it and come back to what your heart feels. My parents never said I love you unless I said it first and that bothered me. You should never get enough of saying 'I love you' to your children.

Get out of the mode of 'superwoman' and allow yourself to enjoy life. We cannot be both parents to our children. Don't raise your children alone. Get out and begin to date, to find a mate and get married. My son needed a mentor even if it was the new man in my life.

Please don't exclude the father out of pride. Even if the father does not support your children financially, having him around means more to a child than money. There have been instances when women say, 'I do not need my son's father to take care of him' and that is a huge mistake to make. You are allowing him to relinquish his rights too easily! My son told his father that he would be homeless with him in the streets just as long as they are together!

It's effortless to get a woman pregnant, but the challenge is stepping up to the plate to raise your children. Enjoy your children with or without the father. It's okay to show your vulnerable side because no one is exempt from problems. It will only benefit your children to see the reality of life. Tell them the truth. The reality today is that most single parents are struggling.

Although I will never trust my ex-husband again, it's more important that my son see him for the man that he is right now. I never told my son anything negative about his father. As he became an adult, he made his own assessment about his father. We are responsible for our children. Don't allow a bad relationship to ruin how you raise your children.

Children need a relationship with adults that are objective and positive. For those of us who are dating again, this is my motto: Never allow any men to meet your child until it's safe to say that you two are taking your friendship to another level – meaning engagement or marriage. Surrounding yourself around numerous men sends a negative message to your children. Do not demand or insist that your children call another man "Daddy." It is crossing the boundaries. He isn't his biological father and it doesn't matter if he gives him money or lives in the same household. Allow your children to decide what is comfortable for them. As soon as that man leaves you, your child will be upset and his relationship with the next man will be unpleasant, to say the least. Then that man will not only discontinue from giving you support for your child, but most stop communicating altogether. If you have a child with him and he has volunteered to support your other child who is by another man that too will stop at some point. It doesn't matter if his biological father is in prison, dead or living in another state, that's his father. Be sympathetic to the decisions you make for your children's sake. Did you have a problem with him while you two were sleeping together?

If you have a daughter, it's not safe to expose her to men that could ultimately disrespect and misplace their kindness. It happens when we look the other way. We expect too much from men who we do not know well enough to trust with our daughters. We begin to leave our children alone with strangers.

Imagine your son sleeping around and calling women unacceptable names. You must be careful that he doesn't think that it's okay to be unfaithful or mislead others. Keep the peace with your ex-husbands or children's fathers. It's crucial that the two of you always communicate effectively and respectfully.

With the growing population of gangs today, teach your children what to do if a gang member approaches them. Make it clear to them to seek help when they are confused about something. Express to your children that the gang is not their family. Manipulation draws you in to this madness.

I learned that although my life with my ex-husband was over, my son must have a clear pathway to him. As an adult, he must build his relationship with his father without me. If his father doesn't act like a father or daddy, there is nothing I can do now but pray because life is too short to carry someone else's sins or burdens.

When the father of your child receives a pat on his back for being a nymphomaniac, you understand why his family treated the 'side chick' and the 'illegitimate child' like his family. Who were the real role models in his life? My son suffered and created bad habits without structure or guidance from his father and extended family.

In my heart Raymond Jr will always be my little son even

if he is 6'6 in height. Once you have children, you will want to step in and make it all better. My son has said many times that he is happy that I have never stopped loving and supporting him even if I did not agree with his life choices. He says that he thought that parents should not ever give up on their children even if they are now adults. Everyone makes mistakes and no one on this earth walks on water. Do not play that 'we are friends' relationship with your children because it could back fire.

"Being an entrepreneur is more than saying it. You live it and it becomes a part of your lifestyle. If you love something so much that you would do it for free, it is a passion! If you love something and you will only do it for money, it is a job!"

(Yasmeen Abdur-Rahman)

"You know you have progressed when you do something without regrets."

(Yasmeen Abdur-Rahman)

"Degrees are helpful, but they won't guarantee you success in the business world. Only faith and dedication to your vision can do that."

(Russell Simmons)

"There is in this world no such force as the force of a man determined to rise."

(W. E. B. Dubois)

"An artist must be free to choose what he does, certainly, but he must also never be afraid to do what he might choose."

(Langston Hughes)

Chapter 13: Owning Your Own

The first money I ever earned was at The Friendly Fuld Neighborhood House in Jersey. My grades in high school provided me with the opportunity to participate in a work-study program. I landed a job as a Clerk Typist/Receptionist to a director. This is where I met a wonderful woman named Mrs. James. She was a role model to me and many of the children in the inner-city projects. She spoke positive and enlightening words of wisdom to the staff.

The job was beneficial because it provided me with the concept of what it was like to receive a paycheck, to work hard, and provide for myself while in high school. It gave me the opportunity to open a savings account and save up money for a rainy day. Mother taught me about independence, survival, and how to set my own goals.

My sister-in-law worked in the human resources department at Ciba Pharmaceuticals (which later merged and is now known as Novartis) in Summit, New Jersey. After graduating from high school and business school, a few years later in October 1989, she directed me to the right person to see for employment opportunities. I landed a lucrative position as a temporary Administrative Assistant. As they say, it's about whom you know when getting good jobs. My career at Novartis helped me to reach my monetary goals while saving up an abundant amount of money within my 401/K account. In addition, it awarded me knowledge of how to use the skills obtained from business school and high school towards organizing and establishing my own business.

Entrepreneurship is like birthing a new baby into the world. If you have a baby, you can appreciate what I am talking about, right? You are passionate about this idea and it takes on its own creation. It begins at the baby stage and then blossoms off and matures to another level. You try to explain your business goals to your family and friends, but the words won't come out clearly due to your excitement. You instantly begin to feel energized talking about how your business ideas began and at times, you will find yourself stuttering because your heart is beating rapid with enthusiasm. This just doesn't happen to everyone.

The entrepreneurial itch has been a part of my spirit all my life. It's great to collect and earn a paycheck from corporate America, but it's an awesome reward to mold your vision into a business. Corporate America loves 'yes' people – those who don't rock the boat. As an entrepreneur, you speak for yourself and affect your own future. Beginning with a vision or a dream of success is major to an entrepreneur. Your vision, drive and dedication take you to the ultimate success of running and operating a business.

While working a full-time job back in the early 90's, it didn't take long to acknowledge my capabilities of providing more than typed presentations, answering phones and making copies of reports. A supervisor in my department asked me to type up a 50-page report. He requested that the report be completed at my leisure. I took the report home and typed it overnight. My supervisor was flabbergasted at how quickly the report was typed and without errors. He whispered to me, "Yasmeen, have you ever thought about starting your own business?" Here is where my entrepreneurial journey began. The thought of it lingered on my mind for weeks. At first, the idea gave me anxiety. There was uncertainty of where to begin this journey. At that time, the Internet became my mentor and the best place to do my research. The bookstore is where I went to pay attention to and take notes on how to run and operate a home-based business. I purchased a few books and later received a recommended list to check out.

Since I have a passion for typing, it was advantageous to start a word processing business. With butterflies in my stomach and jittery nerves, "Yasmeen's Secretarial Services" was born. To maximize my living room space, it was necessary to convert part of my space to an office. My first purchases were an armoire, printer, fax machine and computer. My living room became my home office. Business cards, brochures and rate sheets were created from my word and desktop publishing software. Creating a website was easier than I thought it would be, especially because

I did not have any design experience. The process was straightforward as my job was to enter information at designated areas of the web pages. Afterwards, I went online and sent out an email to everyone, including family, friends and co-workers about the launch of my new business. At the beginning, my services included typing straight documents, reports and creating business stationery (business cards, post cards, and brochures) for my clients. As my skills progressed, additional services were added: pro se (uncontested) divorces for residents who were married in Jersey and life coaching. The divorce idea started as it was necessary for me to seek advice from a close friend about how to process the paperwork. This service was an immediate victory because many people desperately wanted a divorce but could not afford the high-priced lawyer fees. Another service that won over my customers was résumé packages. Weekly, customers emailed me right before an interview because their résumés were outdated and needed my touch. I have seen some résumés that were hand-written and used to apply for positions and distributed during interviews. It's amazing how some people negate the importance of a professional résumé when applying for a job.

A business is founded by your creative thoughts and your passion to pursue what you love. It's your vision. Unlike getting up every day going to a 9 to 5, believing that you can make a living doing something that you have a passion for is remarkable. You tend to daydream about your business all the time. While at work, it was hard to stay focused. Although my body was physically at work, my mind was at home in my office and at my laptop. While walking the hallways of my employer, my cell phone was on vibrate and my home calls were transferred to it. There wasn't a chance that any of my calls would be missed during the day.

Planning ways to market and advertise my services was constantly in my head. Throughout the day, emails were strategically sent out that contained motivational quotes, tips and business promotions. My clients are all at various points in their lives.

Business partnerships can be a success. It can enhance your entrepreneurial understanding and create a buzz as well.

If you two have diverse skills that merge to form one business, the end result can be awesome. More importantly, the two of you must be able to work together and respect one another's opinions. There must be mutual admiration throughout this partnership. At one point, I ventured out with a business partner. My girlfriend and I shared a huge passion for business. We put our skills and experience together to form "The Brownstone Workshop." For weeks, we contemplated what to name our business and how we would divide the responsibilities. At first, because we generally worked alone, it felt weird and wonderful making decisions with someone else. Her vision and creativity linked with my skills and experiences. It was astonishing to throw ideas out to someone who I could relate too. We successfully ran the business together until my business partner relocated to Atlanta. She returned to her previous passion and I continued with "The Brownstone Workshop." Our partnership allowed me to become confident and assertive in my passion for business. My advice is to create a legally binding contract, specifically if money connects the both of you to forming the business.

    You begin to write a business plan based on your feelings, how your services will help your clients, and the drive to make money so that you can branch out into other avenues of business. Before realizing that a business plan was crucial, everyone assumed that we naturally knew how to run our business. While beginning to write my business plan, it became obvious that my passion ran deeper than words. Writing down different sections of the business plan opened my eyes as to how important this venture was to me. What a process to start without a mentor or coach! Writing a business plan is much harder than anyone could envision. This document is necessary to edit constantly because your vision will change all the time. It's a working document. Do not be intimidated by the process. There are places where you can go, for example, hire a life coach, such as myself for advice or seek an expert who writes business plans for a living. On the other end of the spectrum, there are successful business owners who have never written a business plan. They say that it deterred them from pursuing their dreams. So, in saying that, do not get too exhausted behind creating one if you believe that you can display and communicate how your passion will benefit investors or the everyday people that contact you for your products and services. If you are looking to bring in venture capitalist or seeking a bank loan, that plan is crucial.

It was exciting to discuss my business ventures with family and friends. Unfortunately, they would say, "Oh, how nice" and then return to the topics of their careers; what happened on their jobs or in their relationships. It bothered me enormously, but I never complained to anyone about my discouraged feelings. My friends and family rarely speak about my business. It turns out to be depressing when you embark on a business project or gain new clients and no one seems to be at all excited. Only a few of my friends approached me to provide my services. Getting support sometimes is rare.

When my friends are overwhelmed with their corporate jobs, in the back of my mind, I am thinking about running my business full-time. Getting excited about my corporate job just doesn't happen for me; it's simply a job. It supports my business endeavors and pays the bills. In the end, you know that you are the captain of your own personal cheering squad. There were times that going to work with a headache became natural. When opportunity knocks for me to run my business full-time, trust me, there will be no second-guessing. This is one challenge that I am happy to embrace.

Working from home is a great way to operate a business. If you have small children, this option allows you to be available for all or any situations that may arise. Combining an office within my house is convenient for my clients too; however, most times, they meet me at a nearby bookstore or coffee shop. It's convenient because my laptop is readily available to show my work or edit a document immediately while the client is in my presence. One big advantage is that I do not pay for office space that requires utilities and monthly rental fees.

Entrepreneurship should be heartfelt and not pushed on you. There must be a passion for it and a type of love that you sustain without question. It takes up all your time, so why not love what you do, help others and make money doing it? The passion that you have doesn't have a timeframe. There are times while sleeping, the thoughts would wake me abruptly and I would reach for my journal on my nightstand. It's as if my brain never sleeps because of constantly thinking of what to do next for my business. A notepad was even placed on the passenger's seat of my car just in case a thought needed to be recorded.

Along with your passion, there is a vision that others may not comprehend. However, the vision must be clear so that your clients get it. Clarity and confidence are two keys to success. People tend to follow those who are clear about what direction their business is going and how their products or services will help them grow. Always be proud of your ideas and promote your vision to the end. When you're starting out, focus on one vision at a time. Brand your passion and watch it grow.

My coaching services is one of the reasons why 'The Brownstone Workshop' exists after twenty-five years of service and counting. After all the trials and tribulations, my passion is helping others to achieve their business and personal goals. Without a doubt, my services give me great rewards, not only monetarily, but more notably because of my love of giving out beneficial advice and directions in business and life in general. When my clients meet with me for the first time, most are not sure at what type of business to pursue. It's just a matter of clarity that they don't have which allows them to design their vision. My job requires asking the right questions, to see their vision and to facilitate a plan. While at the same crossroads back in 1993, my head was full of so much information. It was necessary to put everything in perspective so that my clients understood my vision and concepts. It's an exhilarating feeling to support someone else because entrepreneurship is my passion. My clients get 100% of my attention. I love to see others with that same drive and determination start their own businesses. Although initially becoming a life coach for entrepreneurs was in the forefront, helping individuals is just as important. I began coaching individuals with personal issues. Some people have anxiety and suffer with depression. Some individuals have families, a corporate job and run a business. I have experienced the good and bad of them throughout my journey.

Writing résumés is my other outlet to helping others reach their goals. Whether you're unemployed, employed, retired, an entrepreneur, new college graduate or student, it's important to have a professionally written and formatted résumé. It should be ready and available for all opportunities. Without this document, you can't apply for open positions, especially if you have a situation where you're fired or laid-off your job. Even if you have a job and an opportunity opens for you, this document must be ready to be emailed or handed to the right person. It amazes me how many people do not have an updated résumé saved on a flash drive or on their hard drive.

There are sacrifices that an entrepreneur must make to become successful or reach your goals. There were times when my girlfriends wanted to talk on the phone, but my clients expected their paperwork completed by the end of that day. There was a time when my son had a project to type up for school. I rushed to help him with his project to cater to a client. A week's vacation from my full-time job was sacrificed to finish a project. When you're a business owner, your hours are unlimited and flexible. If you want to accommodate your clients, most times you're providing your services at unconventional hours of the night. When you want to take a vacation, it surely needs to be planned to the letter. When entrepreneurs are on vacation, it's harder not to answer emails or check your messages. We don't have sick time and vacation time. We are the owners not the employee.

It seems as if my creative juices happen around the early part of the mornings. Since I am an early riser, I'm at my desk 30 minutes before start time. Once at work, I am exhausted. No one understood why I was tired or why I was up late and up early most days. It's important not to speak about my business around management because I did not want to jeopardize my job. This is where my coffee habit formed because I needed a burst of energy to perform my work duties. However, as soon I returned home for the day, a boost of energy came across immediately.

I believe people are where they are today because of divine intervention. Allah laid out a plan for us and we are living it. Some of us are doctors, lawyers, and nurses, but others are running businesses either at home or storefront establishments. The entrepreneurial itch does not happen for everyone.

It has been my experiences to see that most of us stay at jobs for over 10 years and then began to feel uneasy getting up for work. You start to feel like there's something else in the universe for you. I sometimes questioned what Allah put me on this Earth to do, my calling. Your 9 to 5 begins to feel like you've joined the Army. Sometimes when you're at work, you want to be invisible. I get upset when my supervisor is micro-managing me because I am too independent and experienced for that nonsense. This is probably how other entrepreneurs are living out their corporate life right now. I knew that my heart was not there but I had to earn a living. Most entrepreneurs supplement their startup businesses with their corporate paychecks or 401/K retirement plans. Perhaps my business plan will land a venture capitalist one day.

While there are times when business is moving forward and money is coming in from all directions, there are times when business is slow. Keep a marketing plan nearby. I constantly sat at my laptop thinking of ways to market my business. Sometimes running an ad in the paper was costly. I began to reach out to other business owners for strategies. Going to post offices to post flyers, updating my website, sending out introduction packets to newly-opened local businesses and providing presentations were a few of the ways my marketing strategies kept me afloat. When you have satisfied customers, they become a huge marketing tool for you. Always give them a little more than they're paying for because their gratitude will keep you in business. References, reviews and referrals are other ways that business owners advance in their clientele. One hand washes the other. I'm a firm believer that 'word of mouth' works. Today, social media is a 'free' marketing tool. I have continued to land many new clients based on my Facebook business page.

When announcing a new service to my customers, right away my mind begins to fill with anxieties. No one wants to fail at what they love. A client called asking me to create a presentation on how to operate and run a business. Immediately my mind went on overdrive. Creating PowerPoint presentations come easy to me, but when you're trying to showcase what you do, it seems much harder. It helps to get your friends involved. One of my best friends was called to review and edit my presentation for me. In the meanwhile, another friend was called to be my assistant; she helped with the slides during the presentation.

My first speaking engagement was at a local church in North Carolina. As we approached the church, my heart was racing and my forehead was covered with sweat. Everyone was excited and gracious. They saw me as an expert in my craft. Coming there, of course, I did not feel that way, but I am an expert. My confidence level going there was totally opposite when I left the church. There was brunch prepared for all that attended the presentation. The leader of the organization gave a quick introduction of me. I graciously approached the podium. It was an enormous feeling to be in front of people who wanted to hear what I had to say about business. They raised their hands with many questions throughout the presentation. They took notes. They were pleased and impressed.

Although I dressed the part with my tailored business suit and handouts for the audience, this was my first presentation ever in front of anyone. I quickly added this service to my website and edited my brochures as well. This presentation lined me up to participate in yet another workshop later that year.

Sometimes we need to go back to school to carry out our ultimate dreams. While working your corporate job, renew that found energy of entrepreneurship. Coming into your industry with a degree or certification will grab attention from your business partners and clients, but experience is just as important and beneficial. It was obvious to me that going to business school helped with creating business documentation, learning the important aspects of how to run a business, and the expectations of a business owner. Once you take what you've learned and it becomes hands-on, everything falls into place. When you're an entrepreneur, you're constantly learning new ideas and ways to stay on top.

Now I understand what thinking 'outside of the box' means. Even when you begin your journey of running and operating a business, open your mind to other options. At times, go outside the business plan and take risks. It's important to take risks to expand the possibilities of becoming an entrepreneur. All the knowledge that you gain won't come from reading a book. It's not that clear and stress-free. There's room for trial and error. Once you have branded your specialty or written books, your peers and the public see you as an expert.

Stay focused on your goals, not on money. Money is the fuel to move your business forward, but it should not be the only focus when starting a business. At first, most people start with the notion that they can make a certain amount of money and become successful. The first few years, you will feel growing pains of becoming a business owner. I recall reaching out to everyone, but scarcely receiving returned calls. Making cold calls weren't one of the exciting moments for me. There had to be a plan to get back the monies that was put out to start my passion. I began to use my skills to recharge my business. At this point, other services were added to my list. It's necessary to branch out to keep some type of income coming in and new clientele. I mapped out a plan of action. I sat down and wrote out a list of services I could perform to enhance my business profile. A marketing strategy was created and updated constantly. A few of my services were grouped together and others were deleted when they did not fit well with the bigger picture of The Brownstone Workshop.

LIFE LESSONS:

Be yourself! People draw to those who are truthful. If they believe in you, most times they will believe in your vision. People will not co-sign anything unless it makes sense and they can say for themselves that it's the truth. If they see how dedicated and forthcoming you are with your products or services, they will feel like it's worth the risk.

You are never too old to pursue your dreams! Growth doesn't stop with age. Start the process and keep moving ahead regardless of the obstacles you may possibly face. If it means that, you lose a few friends along the way, or take that risk of leaving corporate America, just do it! You will never succeed unless you take the chance and the risk at success. If that doesn't work, try something different. Believe in yourself – if you don't, who will?

Someone once told me to keep a Plan B tucked away. Society tends to revolutionize frequently. Just like trends, business has that same uncertainty. What's hot today isn't hot tomorrow. When you're faithful to your passion, continue to find ways to keep it updated so that it fits your clients' needs.

Do not second-guess yourself. If the entrepreneurial itch happens to you, go for it! Create a plan. Research your topic and begin small. Seek a mentor or someone who is running the type of business you're interested in opening.

Calculate how much money you will need to save up to pay your bills and maintain a business. Decide if you will open a storefront location or work from home. At first, it may be beneficial to work from home. Once your business takes off and cash is coming in, re-evaluate your business plan and take the next step. Some business owners think that they must meet the criteria of other businesses to be successful.

If your friends and family don't see your vision, stop talking to them about it. Join organizations and find a circle of associates who share your business creativity and vision. My friends fall into several categories. There are those who go to the mall with me, talk business with me, and those who just want to talk about everything else under the sun.

You will find that as your business evolves, you'll need to change the structure of your business. Don't be anxious to grow too fast. Again, research your topic. Go to the library and Internet for information.

Remember to purchase professional stationery for your business. At first, I created business cards from my printer. Later, it was necessary to hire a professional designer or use Vistaprint. Your clients will see how serious you are when you pop out your business cards. The stationery will reflect you and your business. Don't give out business cards that have stains on them or those with outdated information. Don't scratch out a phone number and write in the new number; get new cards.

In the end, go for it and don't stop until you reach your goals. Be all you can be and never take 'no' for an answer because 'yes' will eventually come.

"Religion is practiced by people every day; in a church, masjid or synagogue. It is a guide for us to use throughout our daily lives. To others, it pushes extreme worshippers to drive people to harm one another. Use common sense when you read the Qur'an, Bible or Torah but more importantly do not become an Extremist."

(Yasmeen Abdur-Rahman)

Chapter 14: My View on Islam

Growing up, religion was customary in my household. When Mother and Daddy met, she was practicing Christianity. Mother went to church and listened to gospel music all day long, seven days a week. Today, when hearing gospel music, Mother comes to my mind. By the time they were married, Mother began to follow the teachings of the Nation of Islam (NOI), like my Daddy. They were born and raised in Dothan and Abbeville Alabama. My Daddy joined the Nation of Islam at an early age.

Daddy's attraction to the rigorousness of being healthy, groomed, while having a strong sense of Black power moved him towards the NOI. He traveled to Chicago to attend many events that involved Malcolm X, Minister Farrakhan, Elijah Muhammad and other influential men. As a family, we attended weekly, religious functions at the mosque. Mother positioned herself at the mosque. She baked delicious homemade bean pies and scrumptious carrot cakes. Bean pies are made from navy beans. It's a custard, type of pie. These things are synonymous with the NOI. Ordering a bean pie from a sister today is a part of the 'norm' for me. When people think of the NOI, they think of bean pies, bow ties and the "Final Call" newspaper. We didn't consume anything that contained pork. Therefore, Mother cooked lots of fish and chicken.

The women (sisters) wore long white dresses that were called 'longs' because the skirts touched the top of your shoes. The men wore fashionable suits with bow ties, no beards, all clean-shaven and close haircuts. You could spot a brother from the NOI a mile away by his clothing, demeanor and conversations. People said, "They were clean as The Board of Health."

At that time, several of my family members followed the same viewpoints of the NOI followers. Most of the people in my neighborhood were either a Christian or a Muslim. In the late eighties, it became my duty to research the history of Islam. By this time, it became clear that the NOI and the traditional Islamic principles were contradictory.

In 1993, my eagerness and interest in the traditional, orthodox Sunni Islamic viewpoints became what was Islam to me. One day while out shopping at the mall with a close sister friend of mine and her daughters, an epiphany came over me. We made it back to her house, but as we sat on the couch, my immediate thought is that it's time for me to become a Muslim and take my shahada. I took my Shahada (declaration of faith) and became an Orthodox Sunni Muslim. The five pillars of Islam are to profess to: (Faith) There is no GOD worthy of worship but Allah and Muhammad is His last Messenger, (Prayer) Pray five times a day at the prescribed times, (Zakat) Charity, (Fasting) Self-Purification, and (Hajj) Pilgrimage to Mecca, at least once in your lifetime.

Within a week, my hair was covered to signal to everyone that Islam is my religion. Covering your hair with a khimar and body is an act of worship, faith and modesty. I woke up one morning and went to work in my khimar. It was as if a celebrity had walked through the corporate doors. No one at work looked like me so quite naturally when walking through the hallways, people thought that Cancer took over my body or today was a bad hair day. It's inspiring how quickly Islam touched my heart because covering my hair became part of an instinct. To most women, especially African-American women, hair is such a huge part of living in America. If I didn't cover, no one would recognize me as a Muslim. Covering is a part of my life. Prior to my covering experience, while hanging around other Muslims, they didn't know that I was a Muslim. When giving the Islamic greeting, most were a little hesitant or unapproachable. My co-workers respected my religion and within a week, there was another drama going on in the company. My situation was no longer front-page news.

Throughout my transition to Islam in 1993, I legally changed my name to Yasmeen Abdur-Rahman. A brother that communicated with me with the intent to marry began to call me Yasmeen. Curiosity led me to ask him for the meaning of the name. He said that it means – "beautiful flower." Since I am a person who takes charge and knows business, it was my decision to seek out the paperwork to complete the legal name change process. This brought me closer to my religious beliefs and it fits into my religious lifestyle. No, it isn't a must that you change name, but when you research history of Black people, most of us were named from the slave trade.

Calling me Yasmeen was easy, I thought. Muslims, of course, wasn't problematic with the transition. Unfortunately, family and a few of my friends fought against it. They were defiant with my name change. Today, a few family members go back and forth with it, but it does bother me that they don't respect me in totality. Most family members act as if my name change never occurred. My name change reflects my religious identity. The respect of who I call myself legally and religiously isn't respected by all my family members. While most people in the family aren't practicing any religion, they aren't open to people who are certain and definite about what they believe in and how they practice it as well. Today, I know for surety that Allah is in control of everything. What others think or say is irrelevant. Most of the time, I try to bring out the fact that my name is no longer Wendy, but it goes in one ear and out the other. By living in North Carolina, my day to day doesn't involve family members at all. They aren't around me, so calling me Yasmeen would be null and void due to the distance of my presence. It's my right to respond or not respond, and this needs to be checked immediately. Since relocating to North Carolina in 2001, there's certainly not a family presence at all. Regardless, it's about respect. Writing this book opened old wombs. Friends from my past are respectful than my own family.

Then September 11, 2001 happened! Everything seemed great before this catastrophe. The lives of Muslims changed forever. The stares were far more than usual. Over the next few months, it became harder to maintain employment. It was a struggle to maintain my household and sanity. I toyed with the idea of taking off my khimar for interviews because of the discrimination with Muslims after 9/11. With minimal physical support from family and friends, it was a hardship to live in North Carolina covered and giving a fair chance for employment and contracts as a businessperson. What a dilemma!

The safety of my son and I was my priority. There was

a bag in the trunk of my car that needed retrieval on that gruesome day. A carload of Caucasian men passing by yelled out – "I like that turban you're wearing." My immediate reaction was to run in the house. Things turned out to be worse for the Muslims in America. There were numerous, racial and discrimination incidents involving Muslim women and men: a hit and run case of a sister crossing the street in North Carolina; a man spit on a sister on a college campus. Muslim sisters were fired from their jobs; especially those who 'looked like an Arab' and covered their hair. Brothers with long beards were mocked and talked about by non-Muslims.

Before this happened, rarely did America know or begin to understand who Muslims are and what we represent. People didn't know zilch about Islam. Suddenly, people were flocking to nearby bookstores to do research. Google.com had more hits about Islam than any time in history. Qur'an's were purchased by non-Muslims just so that they could get an understanding of the religion; unfortunately, they tried to interpret the Qur'an. The media combined all Muslims and Terrorists into one bag. There are American terrorist from the USA that go under the radar because they're not targeted. Terrorists are also Caucasian (White) me who are a part of the KKK and Christianity. Too much emphasis has been put on foreign Muslims or foreigners in general. Islam is not synonymous with terrorism. Terrorism is not a religion. Islam means peace and submission to the will of Allah. One act of terrorism from Muslims does not reflect the entire religion. Not all Muslims carried out the devastations of 9/11. By the way, did you know that over 1200 Muslims died in the World Trade Center that day? When Timothy McVey, a Christian, bombed the building with all those children, did we as a nation, declare war on all Christians? Did we attempt to burn Bibles? Would you say he's a Terrorist? Yes, he is a Terrorist. There's a double standard in the USA.

After applying for numerous open positions, employers wondered what my ethnicity or religious background was by the name on my résumé. In person, it's obvious that I am an African-American woman. At first glance of my résumé, human resources probably assumed I was an Arab on paper. During interviews, the interviewers barely gave me a strong handshake. It was as if my hands were dirty. There was little or no eye contact during the interviews. They would glance up from time to time but looked away when we made eye contact. Applying for a position that paid a few dollars less than I asked for was not an issue for me. It was necessary to pay my bills and support myself.

By 2003, after 1.5 years of looking for employment, the doors seemed to open for me, but not without a price. After praying for relief, my decision to take off my khimar was a hard decision to make. In my heart, it was an injustice to my religion and my commitment to GOD. Honestly, now I see it was more about what the Muslims would think of me. However, Allah will be the judge of what I do (good or bad). He knows my pain and shortcomings. Everyone has issues to deal with in their religion. My khimar dilemma is not unheard of in the Muslim community. Although, I knew sisters who covered and went out to clubs, that was taking it to a whole other level for me. It didn't make any sense, but again, who am I to judge?

When I attended classes at the masjid in North Carolina, it moved me to tears to see how sisters supported me. One day in Arabic class, the teacher slipped a piece of paper in the side of my pocketbook. I realized later that it was a personal check for $500. I couldn't believe how generous the Muslims were supporting me. She continued to support me a few times over and my heart was heavy. The masjid provided support too and she initiated this gesture. I will never forget this sister and the Muslim community at large.

There were a few Muslim women that I conversed with in Jersey who stopped calling and visiting me. It was obvious it had everything to do with the fact that I stopped covering my hair. It was bizarre because I thought regardless of what I was going through, they would support me. It wasn't a declaration of me leaving Islam or saying that I wasn't a Muslim. In the end, people judged me for taking off my khimar. They were not sympathetic to what I was experiencing as if I had been the first person to go through this type of situation. Where is the sisterhood? Covering is part of worshipping Allah. It does not define whether I am a Muslim or if I'm worshipping Allah less than anyone else. It wasn't my intentions to uncover for vain reasons. My forgiveness will be from my Lord and not from humans.

I am a person who is positive, uplifting and not derogatory and selfish. I don't judge people on what they do, how they look, what they wear or whom they call GOD. All human beings have a purpose in this life. The trials they have encountered on this Earth are their own. This is for Allah to work out because only He has the power to decree our destiny. Allah makes Muslims, not humans.

Islam has numerous concepts and traditions that I love and cherish. For example, the purity and cleanliness are awesome. The ability to pray to GOD directly is another attribute that I love about Islam. Another major aspect is that Muslims believes in all the prophets including Jesus (peace be upon Him). This is a misconception that society and the media has distorted to the rest of the world. If people take the time to research other religions and people they surround themselves with, we would be able to accept others with respect. Religion is supposed to make living easier not hard. It's a way of life and symbol of faith in what you believe in; your existence.

If I cannot do something with full belief and conviction, I rather not proceed at all. The Qur'an thoroughly speaks about hypocrites. There are many Muslims today walking the streets covered from head to toe but aren't praying or practicing Islam honestly. Some men are dressed in their Thoubs (outer garments) and attending Jum'ah (religious prayer) every Friday. Some of them leave to meet their girlfriends or hang out at a club or sell drugs. Numerous times people have asked me why Muslim sisters are hanging out at the clubs covered with a scarf. My responce is that I will not speak for those people and what is in their hearts or their shortcomings. There are times when GOD tests us; some of us fail and others pass with excellence.

I try not to pass judgment on others and decide on what their indiscretions will be for them. No one is practicing his or her religion perfectly because no one is perfect. If we remember that fact, perhaps we can practice openly and honestly without judging others on their shortcomings. Religion should be a way of life, not practiced as a cult. Go to your Lord and repent but repent with good intentions to do better.

When you see Muslims outside of your home and they need your support, do not ask countless questions, help them. While living in North Carolina, the community supported me when unemployment was my test. We must do more to change the distorted images of Muslims. Not because we are scared, only because we must live in peace. Let us be supportive and less judgmental. Pray for each other and stop highlighting each other's shortcomings. Let us go to the media and clarify what Islam means and how most the world is practicing it to the limit. Better yet, be the example of which you seek of others; all religions should follow that perspective and do less preaching.

We are all humans. Whether we are religious or not, we feel pain. If you know sisters in abusive marriages, speak out. Do not turn your head. If you love your brothers and sisters, get them help. I remember seeing a sister with a Niqaab (face covering) lift it up to show another sister how her husband punched her in the face because she did not have food ready for him at dinnertime. Her front teeth were gone. Her calmness surprised and shocked me. She knew not to tell anyone other than her circle of sister friends. Sisters must go to the Imams and put the names of these brothers out there to the public. Public humiliation will curve their behaviors. Stop allowing these brothers to move around without being responsible for their actions. Stop accepting them in marriage just because you do not want to be alone. There is a myth that there is a shortage of good men. Perhaps, it could be the criteria that you have set towards finding the right brother.

There is one male cousin in my family who is an Orthodox, Sunni Muslim like me. I was so happy to share this ultimate lifestyle with him. While growing up, we were close cousins. Our Mothers are sisters, so we're first cousins. Practicing in the same religion, would mean that we would have more in common. In my opinion, my cousin became a fanatic and shed such a negative light of Islam to me as a new Muslim, at that time. He communicated everything that I could not do as a Muslim woman but neglected to report the benefits to balance it out for me. Right now, we are distant cousins. When I temporarily stopped wearing my khimar, he stopped giving me the Muslim greeting. It infuriated me that he assumed that our religion is for his interpretation only. He controlled the topic of conversation always. In his opinion, a woman should have little to say, basically, seen but not heard. Yes, we're Muslim, no, we're not perfect. He was so aggressive that family members would not open the door when he came by to visit them. Or if he called, they would not answer his calls. Allah says not to sever the bonds of family.

We ran into one another at a cookout in Jersey in 2005. As he approached the backyard of our uncle's house with his family, he totally ignored me. This was the first time he saw me without my khimar and Islamic clothing in over 10 years. I am sure this was good conversation on the way home for him and his wife. Yet towards the end of the cookout, he asked me about Mother, but he did not give me the Islamic greeting. Did he not see me as a Muslim? His wife and children were extremely happy to see me and embraced me with love. She never said a word about my relationship with my cousin. It was an unspoken conversation that we did not have about him. He probably talked about me to her but she would not dare get in the middle of it. Every time we saw each other in public, we exchanged numbers but no further communication transpired.

When I saw my cousin again in 2017, the week my mother passed away, he gave me the greetings. No, he never talked to me or asked me how I was doing or anything. Again, the disappointment from a family member.

There are brothers who date sisters and have sex with them without marrying them. Fornication is a sin in all religions. This is a major reason why getting an HIV test is mandatory before marriage. This goes for everyone, not only Muslims. They walk around looking the part but sinning to the ultimate level. Some are sleeping around with other women that are not their wives. Then suddenly, they approach the wives with the idea that someone else is stepping into the circle. After testing the waters, he continues his intimate encounters until he is formally married to the sister. The brother says that he can marry another sister without telling his present wife. Today, most Muslims, depending on what you read, argue this perception or whom you ask, the answer will be different every time. America does not see this as a normal practice, but in Islam, Muslim men can marry up to four wives but most marry just one wife. Let me add that in America, it has become acceptable to cheat with a wife or husband. By the way, in Christianity, the prophets had many wives and the women covered their hair, too. In Islam, it is not mandatory to take more than one wife, but it is allowed.

Some men in Islam tend to use the religion to gain whatever is necessary for them in their lives. For example, it seems as if some Muslim men take the polygyny (plural marriages) to the extreme. Since Prophet Muhammad (peace and blessings be upon Him) performed such acts and Muslims believe he is the closest human being to be perfect by nature, they know that it's almost impossible to maintain or act according at that level of our religion. They quote only the surah's from the Qur'an that suits their needs. Once you do your research and go against what they say, you are now going against everything. Let me add that there are plenty of successful polygyny marriages that are not giving credit in America.

There are many sisters left behind to raise their children while the brother moves on to the next sister. Some sisters do not believe in seeking child support. Some brothers are working dead end jobs and not receiving a paycheck. Some brothers receive his pay under the table. The sister finds it hard to trace his employment history. Then you have those brothers who have lucrative jobs and make the decision about what he wishes to give the sisters. He tells her that going to child support is haraam (forbidden). As the law goes, every time someone has a child by a man in the USA, and then you have a child by him, your support is lowered due to the number of children he legally supports. In my eyes, the total of children the man creates should not decrease the support giving to each child. The amount of support should be evenly distributed. These laws are outdated and need rectification immediately.

When I went to my Wakil (guardian) about finding a suitable mate, he called me with a list of brothers in the community who were looking to wed. Therefore, he set up timeframes where I would meet and greet these brothers. Some of them were engaging and others were not what I considered a suitable mate. This process is necessary because Muslims do not date or meet with a man without a chaperone.

I didn't wear the traditional garb all the time, so there was one brother who thought that I should cover my face. He said, "Oh, I do not want my wife uncovered in the streets – meaning, not wearing a niqaab (face covering)." At first, I thought, I am not naked. It was his mentality that if my face was not covered, I was, indeed, uncovered and the khimar meant nothing without the nikaab. This is another misconception. There are many scholars who differ on this issue. I met another brother who heard that I had a home-based business. He wanted me to work with him in his business ventures. He decided that it would be best not to run my business but regroup and become his secretary. He thought that I should not go out and meet clients, especially men. I knew right away that he would not be a candidate for my husband. Then there was another brother who I began to talk to over the phone. He was my Wakil's friend. He was married with several wives, at that time. My son attended his karate class. Since I was newly practicing Islam, he thought that I would make a great third wife to his already expanded family. He participated in polygyny marriages. At first, I thought, well, this could be an advantage for me because running a business and working a full-time job while raising a son was enough. In my mind, it would be beneficial to have my house to myself and have specific days to cater to my husband. This idea began to weigh in on me. At first, the brother thought that I was too young to venture into this type of arrangement. He thought I was charming and beautiful, yet with a substantial amount of personality to bring to this arrangement as well. He had a huge interest in my son. My son adored and respected him to the utmost. He was an older brother who was experienced with Islam.

As time went on, my knowledge of Islam grew constantly at what was good for me and not good for me. Although he had all the qualities I was looking for in a husband, he brought an overwhelming amount of baggage to the table. With all the children came all the ex-wives and present situations. Sisters seemed happy to bring you into their circles, but jealousy is something that should not be underestimated. We did not marry, but he became a good friend to call on for religious guidance. Everything happens for a reason. Allah knows best.

As you see, it does not matter what religion you practice, no one is perfect and anything can happen. People believe that Muslim women walk five steps behind their husbands. It is a part of jokes that I hear all the time. I honestly do not know what the women in the history of Islam tolerated, but today, I can say that is a falsehood. Let me give you an example of why it would be safe to walk behind your husband. If someone is coming toward you two in anger or to cause harm, your husband would be able to protect you. Muslim women walk with their husbands. Muslim women are publicly working corporate jobs, enhancing their education, raising their children and running businesses all at the same time. According to the history of women in Islam, they were the backbone to men and their husbands. Khadijah actually hired Prophet Muhammad. She was a highly successful woman. Women in Islam should stand up and be accounted for. Let the public know that you are educated and have voices. Let's cut through all the stereotypes that the media has given us. On the other hand, it's great to stay at home and become a housewife and raise your children, too. When we're in public, we must remember how to carry ourselves and be mindful of our speech because we're always being watched.

There are too many interpretations by scholars and that places the worshippers of Islam towards debated issues. Many times, it can become confusing because if you ask a question depending on what masjid you attend, the answers will be different most times. Every year when Ramadan rolls around, the same debate continues. Who fasting on what day and what day is the Eid and what day has the moon been sighted?

The local masjids debate about who is following the religion according to Qur'an and Sunnah. It divides the community because it makes the followers feel uneasy when they visit other masjids. One Imam or followers say that another masjid is not halal. Then the debate tapes surface and rumors begin to flow. This is not Islam.

When you walk down the street and turn up your nose to sisters who are not covered, it's terrible and so un-Islamic. Do you think that the prophets would do that to their brothers and sisters of this religion? We, as Muslims, will remain at war because we're fighting each other to see who knows more surah's or who is dressed like a 'true' Muslim. We can be hypocritical. 'To you be your way, to me be mine' – is a quote from the Qur'an that I follow every day. Allah makes Muslims and not perfect human beings. We are followers and not prophets. All the prophets are dead. We should follow their paths of kindness and forgiveness.

LIFE LESSONS:

I hope my words will touch someone out there who has looked down or said things about other sisters who struggle to practice Islam. I ask Allah to protect us from the hypocrites within and outside of this glorious religion. Be mindful of what you say and how you treat people. The way to Jannah (Heaven) is not by what you wear but how you respect others, how you treat your neighbors, your parents and your obedience to your Lord. Trying to tear down someone else does not make you a better person; it only makes you out to be arrogant.

When you're face to face with a new shahada, be pleasant to them. Do not stuff the whole, entire history of Islam to them in your first visit. Don't try to marry them off before they know how to pray or find out what their rights are as a woman in Islam. If you rush her, she may end up another statistic – a young woman raising children alone without a husband or support.

Take the first step to learn and grow through Islam and not act as if you are exempt from making mistakes. We're all learning this religion and no one is close to being perfect. We are supposed to be reminders for one another. If you see me doing something not of the religion, pull me to the side to explain. Perhaps, I do not know what is correct or going through something in my life that has decreased my level of understanding.

To the non-Muslims, we have more in common than not in common. Get to know Muslims. If you live in a neighborhood close to a masjid, go there and take a tour. If you work with a Muslim, go out for coffee and get to know your co-worker. Ask questions but always be respectful. I love it when people ask me questions about Islam. What I do not like is when people ask a question, I give the answer and then it becomes a debate. I do not debate about my religion. It speaks for itself. You either love me for whom I am because the fakeness doesn't work with me. I am open-minded and an easy person to speak with so be ready for the truth. I don't tolerate disrespect and everyone knows my famous slogan: "Don't let the scarf fool you!"

"A great many people think they are thinking when they are merely rearranging their prejudices."

(William James)

Chapter 15: Black is Beautiful

With all the racism that African-Americans endure, how can we continue to find time to disgrace each other at any given moment? Through Slavery, African-Americans were separated from one another by the color of their skin. Those whose skin colors were of a lighter shade could live inside the 'Big House.' Those who had a darker skin tone slept in the worse conditions outside of the general population: sheds or fields.

During history, the stories changed and for some reason after Slavery was abolished in 1865, today most African-Americans kept the slave mentality alive and intensified. The names that people called me were shocking, especially since they came from someone who looks just like me. It's beyond words how the color of my skin intimidated some people. It's ridiculous to disassociate yourself from others because of the next person's skin color. It distresses me when I hear someone describe another African-American like this: "Oh, I mean the light-skinned girl or that dark-skinned person over there." Call her by her name. We're enslaving ourselves exactly how the slave owners degraded us over 400 years ago.

All African-Americans are intriguing because we share different facial structures, different shades of colors, hair textures, and body dynamics. We still discriminate towards our own people. This topic is exceptionally imperative to address because we must modify our traditions. Those who hide from the facts are foolish thinkers. We must change our thought patterns right now. We have a duty to unify our people. The past will define our future and our children will find the same ignorance in the streets.

A decade of my life, my uncle Fred called me "Darky." Until sitting down to write this book, I did not recognize that it troubled me as much as it does today. My uncle called me this derogatory term as if it was my legal birth name. Although some of the kids in the family growing up with me were given nicknames, mine was offensive.

My uncle loves me without a doubt. My aunt and several other family members are darker than I am but he felt the need to address me with this negative term. It says a lot about him, because calling me 'darky' wasn't offensive to him at all. It's negative to me because of the history of abuse and torture of African-American people and we've gone through enough racism. Strangely enough, another person of color would say this to me. My skin tone and everything about me represents the African-American community and women in general. For me, there are no hang-ups about this issue at all. Black is beautiful.

His reaction to me makes me wonder if he senses light-skinned Blacks have superiority to people of a darker skin tone. Does it have anything to do with his parents and the southern mentality where they lived in Alabama? Most of the southern states are incorporated with the KKK and old plantations. The next time he calls me 'darky,' I am going to pull him to the side and remind him that my name is Yasmeen. Also, let him know how he made me feel throughout my childhood.

There are spectacular shades of what African-American people look like. We should embrace our differences and likenesses. These attributes make us who we are as African-American people. Sometimes I wonder if we're not happy with ourselves, and that it's easier to degrade one another with name-calling. I have heard people say, "Well, I want to marry or have a baby with a dude who has 'good' hair." In the African-American community, that means a brother with straight and curly hair. Hair means everything to us. There is a saying that goes like this: "Beauty isn't solely measured by the length of your hair or the color of your skin. It is your personality, your soul, your heart, and your abilities to give." This says it all for me. In 2019, we continue to be lost and ignorant.

Society brainwashed us to think like this: If you're dark-skinned with long hair, you're beautiful. If you have short hair, you are ugly compared to a woman with lighter skin and long hair. This is such a foolish and immature way of thinking. My hair has been long for at least half of my life, but when I cut it, people said, "Yasmeen why did you cut your hair?" My response was, 'It's just hair.' When my preference is to wear it long, I will proceed to grow it out. GOD has blessed me to be able to cut it short and grow it long. By the way, you will never know unless I tell you because my hair is covered while being outside of my home.

Another note, some think that if you have dark skin and long hair, your hair is a weave (fake hair/wig). Not every dark-skinned woman with long hair wears weave. This is a terrible stereotype. We perpetuate all this nonsense. Therefore, the media plays us for fools. After decades of being 'at the back of bus' we should be positive and stand tall with full self-esteem.

Remembering my high school days, there was a time when everyone was getting a perm or relaxer. It comes to memory of me asking Mother to give me a relaxer. She said, with force, "Why would you want to put a perm in your hair? Your hair is soft and pretty. It doesn't require that you straighten it." Now that I see how Slavery affected most of us, I wanted to fit into that box. Because my hair would curl up and not give me that bouncy affect, just like other girls my age and in my community, I talked Mother into putting the relaxer in my hair. Today, I regret taking such lengths to fit into what others were doing. I am beautiful. What my hair looks like has no reflection on who I am, period.

Sometimes I wonder if I fed into the stereotype of how wearing long hair meant a sign of beauty. While growing up, Black girls equated beauty with long hair. There are those who never cut their long hair because it defines them. They think if the length is short, men would not be attractive to them. There are Black women who will not get their ends trimmed. They are scared stiff that it would take away the length of their hair instead of going through that process to keep it healthy.

One day while watching television and talking on the phone with a friend, we were commenting on an African-American girl. She shouts, "Oh, look at her hair, it must be a weave in her hair." Of course, the girl on television was 'light-skinned' with 'real' long hair. Her comment offended me.

Hair doesn't make or break me. I hope other women hear

me out on this statement. Have you noticed that Halle Berry is considered one of the most beautiful Black women in the world, but for what reasons? She is light-skinned and bi-racial with 'good' hair. Her hair is short. Now, it doesn't matter because she's famous. How thought-provoking is this?

Caucasian women do not distinguish themselves according to their hair lengths. They discuss their weight more than African-Americans do at any given time. We, as African-American women, should expand our thoughts outside of our hood. Take a history course, travel to a foreign country, or speak to people from different cultures, countries and religions.

My sister and I are of different complexions. I remember growing up and some of my classmates saying that she is not my sister because my skin is darker than her skin. Did they overlook the fact that we have the same nose, high cheek bones and lips? How can you look at both of us and say that we're not sisters?

While watching an Oprah Show, the topic was about racism amongst children in America. An African-American, 17 years old, young teenage boy expressed how he was beat up, chased and ridiculed all the time because of his dark skin. He hated himself and asked GOD every day through prayer – why was he born? He constantly thought about committing suicide. His mother was on the show, too. She expressed that throughout her life she experienced that same racism from African-Americans, not people from other ethnicities. When she was pregnant with her baby boy, she prayed that he would not be 'dark.' I was shocked and extremely upset and could not imagine that anyone of African-American decent would think that way of themselves. Did she realize that she was growing and breeding that same nonsense to her son? We are not raising our children to believe that we are extraordinary human beings. Instead, the magazines and television are showing them who is beautiful. We are not the images that society broadcasts all over the news every day. We are not animals. We are such an exceptional reflection of culture and history that no other being will ever emulate. By the way, the teenager on The Oprah Winfrey Show looked identical to my son; tall, dark and handsome.

Another stereotype that I encountered through my experiences is what so many African-Americans say after our children are born. One situation I remember is a person describing her child to me. She said, "Oh, he is dark like his father or light like his mother." My first thought is that it bothers a person that her son or daughter is darker than the other children. Society and Slavery have us thinking these strange things. We fall victim all the time to this nonsense. I can go on for days on some of the things I have heard African-Americans saying regarding skin color, hair textures and other stereotypes.

LIFE LESSONS:

Love yourself and all that GOD has given you. Embrace your lips, your hips, your eyes, your hair and your skin tone. Be who you are without explanations or excuses. Look in the mirror and smile. Do not compare yourself to anyone else. Know that GOD doesn't make mistakes. Being Black is not a mistake! Having dark skin is not a mistake!

GOD created uniqueness and beauty. It doesn't matter if your hair is curly, chemically-permed, nappy, straight – long or short. What matters is that you're a compassionate, respectful and an honest human being with integrity. What matters is that you love people without conditions. What matters is that you defend your culture. What is portrayed in the media is due to racism and ignorance, not logic-thinking people. India.Arie says it plain and clear: "I am not my hair, I am not this skin. I am not your expectations. I am the soul that lives within."

The following is a speech by Lupita after receiving an Essence award:

> "I want to take this opportunity to talk about beauty. Black beauty. Dark beauty. I received a letter from a girl and I would like to share just a small part of it with you: Dear Lupita, it reads, "I think you're really lucky to be this Black but this successful in Hollywood overnight. I was just about to buy Dencia's Whitenicious cream to lighten my skin when you appeared on the world map and saved me. My

heart bled a little when I read those words. I could never have guessed that my first job out of school would be so powerful in and of itself and that it would propel me to be such an image of hope in the same way that the women of The Color Purple were to me. I remember a time when I felt unbeautiful. I put on the TV and only saw pale skin. I got teased and taunted about my night-shaded skin. And my one prayer to God, the miracle worker, was that I would wake up lighter-skinned. The morning would come and I would be so excited about seeing my new skin that I would refuse to look down at myself until I was in front of a mirror because I wanted to see my fair face first. And every day I experience the same disappointment of being just as dark as I had been the day before. I tried to negotiate with God. I told him I would stop stealing sugar cubes at night if he gave me what I wanted. I would listen to my mother's every word and never lose my school sweater again if he made me a little lighter. But I guess GOD was unimpressed with my bargaining chips because He never listened. And when I was a teenager, my self-hate grew worse, as you can imagine happens with adolescence. My mother reminded me often that she thought that I was beautiful but that was no consolation: she's my Mother, of course she's supposed to think I am beautiful. And then Alek Wek came on the international scene. A celebrated model, she was dark as night, she was on all the runways and in every magazine and everyone was talking about how beautiful she was. Even Oprah called her beautiful and that made it a fact. I couldn't believe that people were embracing a woman who looked so much like me as beautiful. My complexion had always been an obstacle to overcome and suddenly, Oprah was telling me it wasn't. It was perplexing and I wanted to reject it because I had begun to enjoy the seduction of inadequacy. But a flower couldn't help but bloom inside of me. When I saw Alek, I inadvertently saw a reflection of myself that I could not deny. Now, I had a spring in my step because I felt more seen, more appreciated by the far away gatekeepers of beauty, but around me the preference for light skin prevailed. And my mother again would say to me, "You can't eat beauty. It doesn't feed you." And these words plagued and bothered me; I didn't really understand them until finally I realized that beauty was not a thing that I could acquire or consume, it was something that I just had to be. And what my mother meant when she said you can't eat beauty was that you can't rely on how you look to sustain you. What does sustain us . . . what is fundamentally beautiful is compassion for yourself and for those around you. That kind of beauty enflames the heart and enchants the soul. It is what got Patsy in so much trouble with her Master, but it is also what has kept her story alive to this day. We remember the beauty of her spirit even after the beauty of her body has faded away. And so, I hope that my presence on your screens and in the magazines, may lead you, young girl, on a similar journey. That you will feel the validation of your external beauty but also get to the deeper business of being beautiful inside. There is no shade in that beauty."

"Depression and anxiety will sneak up on you when you least expect it. Once you realize that you're depressed, get help, ASAP. It will tear you down, make you miserable, and deteriorate your spirit to little or nothing."

(Yasmeen Abdur-Rahman)

"What you see on the outside isn't always what's felt on the inside. You would be surprised when a person is depressed and you have no clue because it isn't about you."

(Yasmeen Abdur-Rahman)

Chapter 16: Coming Out of the Dark

"Going through the motions" is what most African-American women conform to these days. We're enormously perplexed with challenges that shadow our thought progression, our mental state and our ability to function. Many women, in my lifetime, dealt with circumstances that I personally keep close to my heart. They aren't alone. My depression was shielded for years. No one knew how miserable and panicky it felt for me on the inside.

In a recent study of 2,921 single and married Mothers, there was a discovery that single Mothers have a 40% higher incidence of major depression. They have a depressive episode lasting an average of 12 months. (Footnote: "Single Mothers at Greater Risk for Depression" by Dave Turo-Shields, ACSW, LCSW).

Unfortunately, African-American women are undiagnosed with clinical depression often as other cultures. "Our symptoms may not be unique, but they can manifest in culturally-specific ways," explains Kennise Herring, Ph.D., co-author of "What the Blues Is All About." The myth of the strong Black woman only complicates things. African-American women take great satisfaction in adversity. Crying is not a luxury we allow ourselves. African-American women express anger than sorrow. Depression is identifiable as irritability in the African-American community. If you suffer from persistent feelings of pessimism, lethargy, irritability or sadness, it's crucial to seek counseling immediately.

Depression of women in the African-American community is more evasive than other cultures or ethnicities. Most of us won't permit ourselves to seek out professional help. It's taboo to make an appointment with a 'shrink' to discuss our personal business. We're worried about what the next person will assume if we fail to hold it together. Seeming incapable of holding life together is not a 'good look' for us.

Raising a child alone, job stability, inadequate housing, lack of a good boyfriend or husband, and maintaining a financial nest egg have continued to overwhelm us. For me, not being able to get out of the bed most days and avoiding phone calls became apparent. I literally shut down when I heard the phone ringing. Wearing a smile or telling jokes was a mask worn when others were around me. Ironically, people did not see through my mask of trickery. When you are trying to hide depression, it is about making everyone else happy in their space. I am harder on myself than I should be, but I went through this disheartening state off and on over the years.

In the past, opening up to my friends about my financial difficulties was tough for me. There are scores of articles and books in stores on how 'women of color' experience depression every day without knowing it. We go day-to-day being a 'Super Woman.' We pick up our children from school, take them to after-school activities, help with homework, fix dinner and make time to entertain them over the weekends while we work a corporate job and run a home-based business. Especially if you are a single parent, your support system could be non-existent. Lacking support from your parents or family members doesn't make it stress-free.

Most times, crying uncontrollably in the dark while underneath my comforter became second nature. Every love story mentioned to me or when watching a Lifetime movie on television, my emotions reduced me to ruins. Subsequently, my patience would be short. I would 'wild out' on my son without hesitation. Even if he walked in my bedroom to give me a kiss, it bothered me. I knew that I should make an appointment to speak to a therapist, but at the time, the lack of medical insurance decreased my chances to afford the fees. My sanity became writing my book and surrounding one's self with trusted friends and several family members listening without judgments. My friends never said a word and only spoke after my thoughts were clear.

For the most part, people did not see me as being depressed. They thought I was going through the normal day-to-day pressures from work, running a home-based business and taking care of my son. Even though those were things to stress someone out, it was far from the deep depression that tore up my inner spirit. Just because a person shows up for work every day, doesn't mean that they're functional. My depression was concealed for years and no one suspected a thing. Depression isn't a 'real' disease to most folks. A friend of mine said that she didn't know depression was an illness. If anyone at any given time can contemplate suicide that sounds like depression to me. Her statement shocked me to the core. My life was a living illustration of depression; little did she know. When you're depressed, you essentially know right from wrong; it's placing everything into perspective that's hard. When a person says that you're beautiful or they love you – you hear it, but now you must literally feel it, and that's hard.

On a regular basis, my advice helped clients start and operate their businesses. Now, it was my desire to seek help. Everyone assumed that my life was together from A to Z. The reality of it was that my mind and spirit slipped away right before their eyes. Eating became my pastime. Surely, the weight began to pile on. My world was out of control. Although, my body weight and structure were like most 'women of color,' I felt obese. It became uncomfortable over the years to see how my body had transformed. Being thin and trim was my body structure while growing up. When I browse through old photo albums, there are pictures of a skinny person. It created sadness, but it's something to work on. Being skinny isn't my goal today, rather living healthy counts the most.

When people noticed the change in my appearance, my response was, "Oh, this is unemployment weight." There were witty jokes for everything that I didn't want to face head on in my world. When I jokingly told people that I was depressed, everyone laughed out loud with me. They said, "Everything is going to be alright, Yasmeen." It's an overwhelming feeling to be alone while watching everyone around you smile, shop, seem secure and happy. An actor is what I became without professional acting lessons.

My personality became an asset in my life. People expressed to me all the time how they love the aura that I put out in the universe. I love to be in high spirits and make people feel comfortable with me and around me. One key attribute for me is being a positive person. Since my personality caused me to be as positive as I could, while going through the depression, it helped me through the good days. However, on the bad days, my personality veiled behind a gray cloud of sadness.

We put on a disguise every day when we go to work. While sitting in our cubicles, we're thinking about scraping up enough money to cook dinner for our families. We find it problematic at times to come up with enough money to purchase gas to get to work for the remainder of the week. We encompass termination notices lined up on the dresser. We tend to 'rob Peter to pay Paul.' Most of the time, we avoid calls to family members and friends for assistance because we are taught, at an early age, to be independent and not to beg for anything. Asking for help is taboo in the African-American community. When you show people that you're vulnerable or lack money, they see you as poor and unsuccessful.

Most of us believe that money and materials simply are 'successes.' We believe that if there is an expensive ride parked in our driveway, we've made it. On the other hand, if we can 'rock' the hottest brand names every day or look like models on television, we are stylish and unique. What we're doing is covering up depression from the outside and hurting like an uncovered wound from the inside.

Depression comes through the African-American woman from all angles. We find little happiness from other women of color because of the jealousy and intimidations that we create. We do not acknowledge other women who are just as stunning. When we see, a woman walking down the street wearing a funky hairstyle or sporting a fabulous pair of boots, we turn our heads. Instead, envy takes over and a derogatory thought runs through our brain.

Depression makes us either sleep too much, become unresponsive, non-social and at most times, obese. Some of us become obese by supplementing food as a resolution to our problems. Some of us spend money that we do not have because going to the mall would bring short-lived satisfaction. By the end of the week, you'll need to make returns at the store because you have spent the bill money.

Personally, my weight fluctuated up and down over the past 15 years. Dealing with a stubborn, growing teenager, relocating to another state, unemployment and lack of a personal life, I let myself go. This is another avenue that most women take when they are feeling unbalanced and out of control with life. Clearly Allah can change my situation but finding the strength to move forward was hard at times.

When visiting family members, they see you physically and not your pain and say, "You gained some weight." They do not see me and say, I missed you or I love you. My weight became the topic of conversation at every visit to New Jersey. It's depressing to have people watch your weight gain and think that you are fat or obese. Yet, they do not care whether you have a place to live, food in your refrigerator or need support. Most people in my family are negative and uneducated. They have one-sided conversations. I can count on one hand the family members that I keep in touch with today. They have tried to break my spirit but I refuse to let them.

Now that my story is out, people flock to me with their stories. I am not in this alone. We are horrified to tell the truth about our situations; we are embarrassed and humiliated most times. That same point of secrecy will further diminish your world if you don't talk or open to someone you can trust. Help others while you are hurting; it's therapeutic. Through my depression and anxiety, it gave me the ability to write my book so that others could use it as their survival guide.

Depression and anxiety led me to be in relationships with men who I should have turned my back too or never gave them the time of day. We look for a shoulder to cry on and someone to take the pain away. My thoughts weren't about me, but more about how to make someone else happy. The gratification that I had from it was temporary. Depression and anxiety takes away your self-esteem and you feel empty and useless. Depression will allow you to walk in your space as if you are okay, but once an incident occurs, you become the battle between sanity and madness. I can recall crying one day for no reason at all. I could not catch my breath. A vomiting sensation rushed through my body. Then all my emotional traumas that I experienced in my life came to the surface.

A bad relationship seems great when someone gives you a small amount of attention. However, when you come up out of it, you will see why you made certain choices, and how it caused harm to your heart. Once you build up your life again, everything that you depended on will change its' course and the light shines brighter for you.

At forty years old, I felt like a plane gliding through the sky at an altitude unreachable to others. It's comparable to running through the warm sand at a beach with the sun beaming on the back of my neck. It's like cleansing in clean, blue water filled with scented bubbles. It reminds me of how I felt like 'The Mother of Year' when I walked out of the hospital with my brand-new baby boy.

This is a pivotal phase of my life. As a woman, I know this milestone reflects on a carefree and positive life that I lead today. Nothing can touch me now! Now, I am optimistic about the hope for my future. I can grasp a list of goals to reach and conquer them all. Nothing is too far from my reach. No one will deter me from all that I deserve. There was a time when I had to get advice from others before making a critical decision about a relationship, a career move or moving forward in business or religion. At that time, my self-esteem was lousy. I did not see how much of me I could offer the world. When I was younger, I thought everyone knew more than I did. Fear stopped me from making decisions for myself. I stayed in relationships with people who should have never shared my space with me at all.

Surrounded around spiritual and encouraging people makes my day. Sending motivational quotes through emails to my friends, business associates and family members contributes to my spirit. As it gets them through the day, it allows me to stay on the right path. It feels good when you know that others are moving in a positive way. There is no room for fake and disloyal individuals in my life. When I looked out the windows of the eighth floor in Hayes Homes Projects, I wondered if people thought I was poor and trashy. Now I care less about what the next person thinks of me as a person, my religion or my stand on politics. It doesn't matter if you disagree with me or do not understand where I am coming from when I express my opinions. I am not looking for a handout nor will I second-guess my feelings ever again.

Today, I realize that life is incredibly precious. Working more than my share of time in corporate America, shows me that it's more than getting up and going to work. It's great to enjoy the money you make and the time put into achieving it. At this point, we now know that there's more out there than working a 9 to 5. What is the whole process worth if I don't take myself from it every once and a while?

It is astounding how many people young and old call on me to give them advice. Although most of them have taken different roads that I have traveled, they managed to dig themselves deeper into a world spin. Some say that my heart is huge and my soul is like an older woman of wisdom. I feel like I have lived a long life. Perhaps that is true, depending on whom you are talking to and what environment you come from in your world. When I give advice about relationships, it is honest and realistic. When asked about raising a son alone, some people just don't get where I'm coming from. Some become silent after my statements, and others piggyback my thoughts. After going through several dysfunctional relationships, my advice is sweet and simple. For sure, my experiences don't mean that the next person will go through the same path that was chosen for me. They see that even with a smile, we can hide our fears and emotions. When you're confident and positive, you take the good with the bad and continue to keep motivating thoughts on the rest of your life.

When talking to various younger people, especially women, they seem so indecisive and unstable. For one, I wasn't like that when I was younger. Some of us mature faster than others, but unfortunately, those who do not mature fast and make the wrong choices will find themselves repeating the same mistakes that other women have made, too.

My past won't determine my future. My past will allow

me the understanding and maturity to be a better person and too be able to become a better wife and mother. When you're married at a ripe age of 21 years old, some aren't ready for such a defying task of becoming the other half of someone else. Take my advice and set goals, accomplish them and allow your maturity to speak for itself. Don't rush maturity; let it come naturally.

A Facebook friend expressed this thought: "Most people who don't have anxiety or depression don't get it. They don't understand what you mean when you say you cry for no reason. They think you're just emotional. They don't know how it feels to have your heart pumping out of your chest. And to be short of breath and can't control it, or to feel like the whole world is tumbling down on top of you and you can't fix it. They don't get that anxiety and depression are both illnesses, not a birth defect. They think we like the attention, but they have no idea how badly we want to feel happy. To have a real smile, not a fake smile; to not go through the day feeling worthless; to not cry for a week straight; to just be happy, like the average human being should be."

LIFE LESSONS:

Growing up in a family that does not say, 'I love you,' is tough. How would they know that I was depressed and dying on the inside? Family should be your first step in the direction of support. You should be able to find discretion and a shoulder to cry on especially when you are going through hard times. Even when you want to tell someone that you achieved a goal, they should be on your side, appreciate your successes and not shoot down your dreams.

Depression and anxiety comes in many forms. When you are not as social as you used to be, or when you begin to stop taking calls or wanting to get up for work, get help!

Create a sister circle. When you sense yourself falling into a funk, your instinct is to withdraw. Consistent bonding with your girlfriends is like Wellbutrin for the spirit. "Humans are creatures of community," says Upton. We are healthiest when we're surrounded by loving people and in loving relationships. Call on your clergy, your parents, or your significant other. Perhaps, the people who are closest to you will see that you have changed.

Trust those whom have your best interests at heart. Depression and anxiety, makes you feel uncomfortable and embarrassed when it hits you. Take time for yourself. Do not overextend yourself. Do not give up on who you are and what you represent. Give yourself credit. Like the title of E. Lynn Harris' book says, "And This Too Shall Pass."

Embrace your age. Love the skin you're in and move forward with grace. Take heed to the life-lessons and indulge in good, positive conversations. Make your time meaningful to you. Appreciate yourself. Love from the inside out. Spend time alone and regroup from day to day. Don't allow others to run your life. Leave work at work. Follow your dreams by pursuing your passion. It's never too late to grow. When someone agitates you, confront this person immediately. Don't wait for the next time because the next time may not happen. If one door closes, remember another door opens. Every day that you keep a frown on your face, your enemy wins. The Devil is real!

"If we have unyielding faith while moving steadily toward our intentions, all that threatens us along the way will go into hiding."

(Susan L. Taylor)

Chapter 17: Dear Mama

April 12, 2017 will go down in history of being one of the worse days of my life. My mother passed away unexpectedly on that day. As I drove on Highway 40 in Raleigh, NC coming home after a long day of working overtime, I looked up to see the call. It's a number from Jersey. I'm thinking it's either a family member or someone calling about business. The caller identified herself as a nurse from Saint Barnabas Hospital. She requested a number of my family member that's locally in Jersey. I gave her my Uncle Franklin's number, Mother's baby brother. The nurse hung up quickly without any explanations. Mother was a slender, exceptionally physical and healthy lady in her late eighties. So, there weren't any bad thoughts that came over my mind. Since I was literally 15 minutes or less from my job. I made it home quickly.

As I'm walking up the stairs to my front door, my uncle calls to say that he and his wife were on their way to the emergency room. His wife doesn't go to hospitals or anywhere near sick people, period. She suffers with depression. She waited in the car for my uncle and Mom to leave the hospital. The nurse directed my uncle to wait in a room for the doctor to speak with him regarding Mother's health. Even at that moment, my thoughts were calm, cool and collected. Uncle Franklin put me on speaker phone when the doctor entered the room. He said, 'This is my niece from NC on the line. My sister is her mother. She needs to hear the details of what's going, too.' The doctor said, "Sorry, but she didn't make it. She didn't suffer or bleed internally." Uncle Franklin yelled out and his phone dropped to the floor. Did I hear what I thought I heard? My mother was dead. My uncle hung up and called me back after viewing Mother's dead body. I remember saying to him, "What happened?" Why is she dead Uncle Franklin? He's a jovial person; always happy and telling jokes and joking around. He was crying! He said that her face was swollen.

Uncle Franklin would be the first person for me to call in regards to Mother's health. I knew that he wouldn't hesitate to check on Mother. He has been the caregiver in my family for several family members. Just think, my auntie, my mother's baby sister, died one month prior to Mother's death. Uncle Franklin took care of my aunt for years leading up to her death. Now, he's looking at another sibling dead in the hospital. I felt horrible for him because he and my mother were extremely close. She spoiled him rotten. Mother was like his mother and she took care of him as if he were her son.

One month prior to my Mom's death, I remember talking to him while he was cleaning out my aunt's apartment after her death. I recall in our conversation saying to him – "OK, now you must look after my mother. She trusts you. I'm not there to watch over her day to day health and living conditions. He says, "Yes, I know. I'll be here for her just the same as I did for my other sister." He had that confident, I'm the big brother attitude that made me smile.

After hearing this disturbing news, I began to walk around my living room in circles. I was in shock. I recall saying, "I can't believe she's dead." Less than 72 hours ago, we talked on the phone. She told me that she was cleaning out her refrigerator. To some people, playing videogames is a passion. For Mother, cleaning was her ultimate passion and she pursued it with avenges. Her cleaning habits rubbed off on me. I'm OCD and some people, like my husband can't understand it. My mother knew where everything was located in her apartment just as I do today in my house. Everything was neatly packaged away. As always, at the end of our conversations, I say "I love you, Ma." Who would've guessed that it would be our last conversation?

My mother was the first person to call when I needed to vent about anything going on in my life. Mother listened to me. When Mother called me venting about our family, it placed me in defensive and fight mode. Sometimes I gave her advice that she disregarded, but she respected my opinions and concerns. She never pushed me to the side. She never passed judgment on conversations that she didn't comprehend. When I asked for her advice, she gave it to me straight and raw. She didn't have a filter. The first thought that came to her mind turned into words from her mouth. Mother was a dependable, loving parent. She stood by me during my marriage, divorce, the birth of my son, medical conditions at an early age, graduations, and my relocation to North Carolina. She respected and admired the religion of Islam and the lifestyle change which made my recognizable as a Muslim. The one and only change in my life that she failed to respect was my legal name change. She and other family members, including my dad refuse to call me Yasmeen. Yes, it's disrespectful because my name is no longer Wendy. I am legally named, Yasmeen Abdur-Rahman. It's funny because there are several people in my family who use Muslim names. They are called by Muslim names and they're not Muslims. Their names are not legally changed. It makes me scratch my head at things that I see and hear especially from my mother's side of the family. It is really up to me to correct the issue head on and not respond until it is out of respect that they recognize my name. I will continue to pray about it but not hold it against them if it is a new habit that they just can't conform to. What I do know is that prayer changes everything. The fact of the matter is that my allegiance is with Allah, not my family or anyone else for that matter.

I remember calling a few of my closest family members to let them know that Mother was dead. My cousin in Atlanta whom I grew up with talked me off the ledge. His mother, my aunt, passed away years ago. He knew that my heart was broken into a thousand pieces. In less than two days, reservations on Amtrak were made for me to get to Jersey to view mother's body for the last time. My husband was working in Pennsylvania and that's where my Amtrak ride ended. We drove from Pennsylvania to Jersey that evening. It had been a few years since my last trip there so this wasn't one of my happy moments. Actually, my last trip to Jersey was a visit to Mother's house for a full week. A dinner event was pre-planned at Mother's house. The invitation went out to my close friends and some family members to meet my husband. We had a wonderful time. My husband and mother spent the day cooking all types of meats and different cultural foods. My husband is Nigerian and loves to cook. We laughed. We ate and socialized with people who loved me. Mother enjoyed us. Everyone took pictures together. Mother had most of the pictures from that visit enlarged at a local CVS store. I found them in her apartment. The pictures had me reminiscing about each and every encounter with Mother that entire week-long visit.

This is the first time I had to be a part of making funeral arrangements for someone. My uncle, aunt, sister, cousin and husband all sitting in a room waiting on the funeral director to meet with us. Strangely enough, Mother expressed to me through many conversations of how she would like her funeral arrangement to be conducted in the event of her passing. We had this conversation on a regular basis. Mother was not afraid of death. Her direct quote was: "Don't spend the money on flowers or an elaborate casket. Please use the money for yourself." Even though I knew mother's wishes, my voice was not heard while making arrangements for her to meet our Lord. People pitched in to say what they thought without any knowledge of mother's wishes, including my sister. It's like no one cared what I thought. It felt as if I was in a conference room full of people who were talking around me but no one could hear me when I spoke. I can guarantee that I spoke with mother 100 times more than my sister or anyone else in Jersey for that matter. Out of sight, out of mind to my family. It was politically correct to suggest the family to be in that room at that moment. Back to being the people-pleaser and not executing what I know is best for Mother. Today, I regret that I allowed them to push me to the side.

My family wanted to get an expensive casket. It was for them and not what mother wanted to be buried in at all. A few days later, the casket I selected was exchanged to the casket that everyone else wanted. My cousin told me that I picked out the "welfare" casket. His unworthy and disrespectful remark immediately had me pause in my spirit. All of these poor people in my family who appeared like they were rich but more like slick with the mouth. This outspoken family member whom I did not have a relationship with over decades told me that I picked out the 'welfare' casket. I had to count to 10 before I reacted to this nonsense. How do you speak those words to someone who just loss her parent? It wasn't about you; it was about my mother. Technically, my sister, dad and myself should have been the only people in that room making her final arrangements. Perhaps, he wanted people to believe that he is the man in town. Plus, both of his parents passed away and would he had appreciated a comment like that from me? The funeral industry is nothing more than a racketeer; making money off poor people especially in the urban, ghetto neighborhoods. It felt like my cousin was in partnership with the funeral director; trying to cut deals as if he was pocketing a kickback for every dead body on his listing. I walked into the lion's den that day!

Regrettably, my dad did not attend the funeral. He relocated back to their hometown of Alabama. It saddened me that he was not there to support me. To have his emotional support would have made my me feel closer to the beginning and the ending of my story; the two people who created me. Yes, he sent money to support the burial, but that was not important to me at that moment. They were legally married even at the time of her death. He should have taken charge of the arrangements as her husband. Yes, they were separated but it's the responsibility you take when you remained married. My parents shared an unspoken love for one another. It upset me because he attended other funerals, just a few years ago, of other family members on mother's side. As a matter of fact, the picture displayed on her obituary was taken at my uncle's funeral a few years ago.

Mother was an Alcoholic. For me, it wasn't something that made me feel ashamed of her because she was sick. Majority of her siblings were and today are under the influence of alcohol and drugs. My grandfather, Pop, was an Alcoholic. It's in her genetic DNA. Although she passed away of natural causes, I know that her history with alcohol played a major role in her demise. We talked about her lifestyle all the time. The conversation of her getting help came up on a regular basis. She admitted to me that she had a problem with alcohol. She down-played the chronic excessiveness. She was hospitalized a few times for alcoholism. She was admitted into temporary hospitalization months prior to her death but legally they were not able to keep her indefinitely. To see Mother during her outbursts were heartbreaking. Mother attended many family gatherings. She was offered and allowed to drink alcohol and that was an atrocious act to me, especially coming from people who claimed to love her so much. My family knew Mother needed help. They contributed to her sickness. My mother was independently living on her own in a nice department complex in West Orange – suburban area of New Jersey. She drank and no one knew it until she started to call the family talking out of her mind or crying uncontrollably. It became a normal routine. People around her remained neutral and stayed away from the reality of her condition. Well, yes, several family members talked about her alcoholism in a negative manner. Even at the passing of my mother, her sister talked about her being an alcoholic sitting in my mother's living room. It took everything out of me not to curse her out. When my mother was alive, my aunt talked behind her back. She called my dad talking about my mother's behavior. My mother continued to help her siblings, especially this particular aunt. She helped her by referring her for volunteer work at several places, baby-sitting her children, and cooking meals for her church events. My aunt spoke negatively about my mother to their boss at the jobs they both attended. My aunt wondered why she never heard my voice at the other side of her phone. How can I call you after you purposely torn down my mother's character and tried to sabotage her while at work? Do you not see how unchristian like you are in my eyes? It is amazing how people who claim to go to church or speak about Jesus, but they tear down other people ever chance they get! What would Jesus think; that's what the Christians says. My mother was hurt by my aunt's way towards her because she told me during numerous conversations. When my aunt asked her to cook something or help her during her many moves in Jersey, Mother never said no. In my honest opinion, it felt like my aunt was jealous of her own sibling. Mother had a way about her that people just flocked to her heart. My aunt was the opposite. She was sneaky and untrustworthy. It's unbelievable to me as an adult to feel this way about her since we were close during my childhood years. She is not the same person from the past. After leaving Jersey to return back to North Carolina, my aunt has not called me to check up on me at all. No, I am not surprised.

  According to my dad, Mother's alcoholic behavior started when she began to party and hang out at bars and nightclubs with her oldest brother. This started before I was alive. This is a story that my dad told me after her death. As I became an adult, the conversation about why they were separated never came up. When practicing the Islamic religion, you do not drink, eat pork or foods that contain pork or smoke. Mother began to do the major sins of Islam. My dad was disappointed in her actions. Mother converted to Islam after she and my dad were married. She was active at the mosques, as she used to call them. She baked bean pies and carrot cakes. Unfortunately, due to the lifestyle changes that Mother presented to dad, their relationship became unhealthy. My dad worked hard on their marriage to keep the family together. Then one day, Mother told him to get out. He never came back.

Regrettably, that trip to Jersey to put Mother to rest rekindled depressing and joyful recollections of my life growing up in Jersey. It was over 15 to 20 years that my family and friends were absent in my life. With some, there were no calls and definitely no visits to North Carolina. When you relocate to another state, people expect you to come back and visit them. I am still waiting on people to come to North Carolina to visit me. The night my husband and I arrived at Mother's house, it was a bizarre feeling. We called the superintendent of her development to get in her apartment. While in her apartment, I didn't want to touch anything. It felt like she was still alive but we were waiting on her to return home. You could smell the aroma of her cigarette smoke or whatever meals she cooked that week. Everything was just as she left it.

When my husband and I were ready for bed, I couldn't see myself sleeping in her bedroom. I slept on her living room couch. The next night, there were sounds coming from the front door. It was as if Mother was putting her key in the door. It was spooky! The next day, I called one of closest friends to see if it was okay to stay with her until the night of the Wake. My husband had to rush back to PA to finish a construction job. He returned the day of the Wake. Going to my friend's house kept me from being alone while taking my mind off my mother for a few days. It felt good to laugh and watch movies; a big distraction that was necessary.

The day of the Wake was like waking up in a fog. I remember walking in Perry's Funeral Home in a daze. It felt as if I was watching from the outside of my soul. My immediate family was there waiting on me. Without looking or talking to anyone in the room, I walked straight to my mother. I kissed her on the forehead and started talking to her as if she was sleeping. The hour that I shared with Mother before everyone else came to view her body was a memory to keep for life. I told Mother how much I love her. I told her that she will be in my heart at last breath. Leaving her side and knowing that it would be forever felt like someone had snatched her away from me. I didn't cry at all. I was happy to see her. It's safe to say that I was still in shock. I can't believe that tears didn't roll down my face as I approached the casket. It didn't feel real. My memory kept bringing me back to our last conversation while trying to remember her voice in my head. Having that time with her meant the world to me. Taking pictures of Mother in her casket felt unreal. As I look back on them today, it makes me feel numb.

Family and friends started coming in to see Mother. Her co-workers from the hospital where she volunteered showed up and supported the family. She was truly loved. Many of my friends arrived to support me. The love and hugs were a comfort to me during this most devastating event in my life. School mates from high school, neighbors from places where we lived and lots of Mother's friends attended her Wake and funeral. It had been decades since not seeing many of my cousins whom I grew up with in my family. Unfortunately, we reunited at my Mom's Wake instead of a family reunion or a happy occasion.

The darkest hour was the funeral. As I began to get dressed for the funeral, I knew it would be the last day that I physically saw Mother. The magnitude of sadness hit me immediately as I sat down in front of her casket. During the funeral, there were times when it felt like my heart had stopped beating. The tears wouldn't stop falling from my eyes. All of the conversations that we had about death suddenly were at the forefront of my mind. It felt like someone had literally took a knife and poked me in my heart. The person in my life who talked to me every day was gone. The person who laughed at my jokes, loved me unconditionally, cooked peach cobbler for me and wished the best for me is gone from this earth.

At the funeral, my husband stood at the podium to speak about Mother. It was touching! It wasn't a planned speech. The two of them spoke on the phone regularly. She talked while he listened. She told him about her issues regarding our family. We laughed a lot about how she tried to say his name. It was hard for Mother to remember his name because he has an Arabic name. It became an inside joke with us. I'd say – Ma, what's my husband's name again? She'd twist it up and we laughed so hard that tears poured from my eyes.

During my husband's speech at the funeral, he described the process of asking my parent's permission to marry me. He talked about how you have to respect your parents even if you don't agree with them. There should never be disrespect towards your parents at all. My husband's support was what I needed to get through this emotional rollercoaster. I'm proud that they had a wonderful relationship. I recall during my last visit to Jersey how we went to Dunkin Donuts for breakfast. My husband opened and closed the door of my car or any car that we're in but Mother wasn't accustomed to that gesture. As we were parking at Dunkin Donuts, my husband got out to open my door. I said – Ma, stay in the car, my husband will open your door. She said, "Oh, that's nice of him; okay, I won't touch the door." It was so cute.

I wanted to speak at the funeral but my heart was shattered. Trying to speak a word out of my mouth would have been the abrupt end to my speech. The world needed to know how much Mother meant to me. For the family members who took advantage of Mother, they will feel the emptiness for the rest of their lives. A lady who was a former drug addict got up to speak. She reminisced on conversations they had and what Mother told her to do to get pass her demons. People whom I never met before spoke about Mother with tears in their eyes. Some people told stories that made me laugh. Mother was naturally a funny person as she became older in her years. She didn't have a filter. Sometimes I would say, "Ma, don't say that or please don't say anything."

Finally, it was the end of the funeral services where each row of people began to get their last view of Mother. I can still see myself getting up to see Mother for the last time on this earth. I wanted to just stay with her, kiss her and tell her that she's missed in my life. Mother's casket slowly began to close. Her phone number is still saved in my cell phone. Unfortunately, her last voice messages were deleted the day before she passed away. I wish I could hear her voice again.

Going back to clean out her apartment after the funeral was uncomfortable. Again, I didn't want to bother her stuff. In the end, my mother's awards – a clock engraved with her name were items that I packed in my suitcase. Mother was extremely clean but she hoarded too much stuff. There was an abundance of things that reminded me of Mother. Today, her clock sits on my nightstand in my bedroom.

A few days after the funeral, anxiety started to creep up on me. It was time to start living again and take my journey back home to North Carolina. My husband and I thanked my girlfriend and cousin for their hospitality and love. My job was done. Mother was at her final resting place. Now the mourning began as I arrived home. Once settled in, mailing out the condolences cards took me back to sadness of the Wake and funeral. I cried and cried for weeks and months. Two weeks after burying Mother, it was time for me to prepare for my upcoming scheduled surgery. After the surgery was over, I was home for a month recuperating in a lot of pain. Out of habit, the contact button with Mother's name was hit in error on my cell phone. She would have come to North Carolina to visit me or called me every day to check up on me. She didn't like to travel as much once she was diagnosed with Breast Cancer years ago. Mother was in remission for at least 10 years.

Four weeks of short-term disability went by and it was time for me to return to work. The first week, as I sat at my desk, tears rolled down my face. Out of nowhere, I started crying. Two years later, I'm still crying. Mother is on my mind every single day. How do you not think about your Mother? How do I go about my day without crying? Now, I truly know the feeling of such devastation of not having my Mother in my life. She's gone.

LIFE LESSONS:

No one on this Earth will love you the way that your parents love you, especially your Mother! Never take for granted the love that you share. Never take for granted the time that you spend with your parents. Mother didn't graduate from college but she was smart. Mother didn't work for corporate America, but she knew how to take care of her family: cleaning houses and commercial offices, a crossing guard for an elementary school, volunteering at hospitals and daycare centers, a bartender at a family bar and other small jobs throughout my childhood. She passed along excellent traits and characteristics that became a part of my growth. For example, you will never come to my house and it's not clean or livable. It gives me anxiety if my house isn't clean to my standards.

As a teenager, I sat in the kitchen watching Mother cook all types of foods. I've wanted to call her to ask how to cook something that she used to cook for me. I wished that my mother would have continued to follow Islam because our relationship could have been even deeper. For example, the way she was buried would not have been an ounce of drama. The funeral would be purely religious, simple and quick. My dad is a Muslim. I pray that he has expressed to his family in Alabama and my sister how he demands to be buried. I pray that they respect his religious beliefs and obligations. This is an obligation that needs to be notarized and copied to all interested parties. I refuse to be a part of my dad's burial and not be heard or seen. He will be buried as a Muslim, as long as I am alive to be there for the arrangements. I was told by my aunt that my sister should be called in the event of his demise. There were many times that it was expressed how important it was to prepare a Living Will.

My mother was a helper. She helped lots of people, including her family, and especially her siblings. When I became an adult, it was my job to protect her and do what I could to make life easier and that's what I did for Mother. Today, there are no regrets in my heart or spirit. Make sure you are doing the same for your parents.

"The reality of faith is knowing that what has passed you by was not going to befall you; and that what has befallen you was not going to pass you by."
(Tabarani)

"If something befalls you, do not say, 'If only I had done otherwise,' but rather say, "Allah's Will be done,' for 'if only' opens the door to Satan's mischief."
(Bukhari)

Chapter 18: Through the Fire: A Woman's Journey

"Through the Fire" is a title to a song that belongs to the outstanding, R&B singer, Chaka Khan. If you know the song, you know that it's both significant and serious. In life, you're going to be challenged and tested. Starting a new business is a risk. Working in corporate America is a risk. Getting married is a risk. Raising children is a risk. Buying a new car is a risk. I challenged myself. The learning process and experiences gets rough. When you're going through the motions, you tend to see things in a different light. All effects may not have a bright light attached to them. Some things aren't as clear as you'd like them to be at that time. The light isn't shining non-stop at the end of tunnel.

There are several stages in my life that I have gone through. In my childhood, growing up in a household with the absence of my dad is the results of how I dealt with men. Often at times, I looked for love in all the wrong places. Getting married to a man who didn't know the actual meaning of commitment and integrity ruined my chances of opening my heart to the right man. Getting divorced opened my eyes and forced me to become stronger and self-sufficient.

Birthing a child into this world means giving advice, structure and direction from birth to adulthood. As a parent, by no means do you stop loving your child. There is an equally separate relationship between us now.

Starting a new business gave me the self-determination to show myself that I can do more than type. Writing this book exceeded all my expectations as a new author.

When I think of going through the fire, I see myself falling without breathing or trying to escape the heat. It's like feeling someone holding on to the bottom of your leg, and not being able to move. Enduring the deceptions of adultery and many other frustrations from my past, I see myself walking away with burnt marks on my heart and scarring on my body. There was a sense of shortness of breath from inhaling through the smoke. There are times when I didn't know which way to turn – left or right. I wondered which friend to turn to when I needed help. Other times, I was unsure which secrets to keep to myself.

I set countless limitations for myself. From time to time, I thought about decisions that should have been made in my ten-year marriage. For example, I should have divorced my ex-husband immediately when he cheated the first time. The writing was on the walls. As they say, it was too good to be true. He was more of a con artist than a charming man. He received everything he needed for his happiness. As his wife, I had the distinct opportunity to carry his last name while being the mother of his named, born son. Strangely enough, he was an immature big teddy bear. He didn't have the tools necessary to be a husband; an example that he should've seen with his dad.

Dating a man who gave me part of his life affected me. Believing that he wanted me to be his wife was hurtful. Now I caught a glimpse of the real person behind the innocent smile and persona. He gained power and I was left behind feeling dedicated to him. Nothing good comes from that type of relationship. I soaked up the dream that he fed me repeatedly. When a person says that they love you, it should be unconditional, or not with limitations. There shouldn't be a compromise on his or her love for you. As they say – ole habits are hard to break.

There are decisions you've made that have rocked you to your core, shaken your soul, and irritated your spirit. You may feel like you've just made the worst decision in the world. You may question your morals, values, and integrity. You may put yourself down and feel like you've made foolish choices. The reality is, even during it all, Allah is in control.

Take some friendly advice from me; a person who has seen, heard and done a few things that I would do over again if I had that type of power. You are not perfect. No one should expect perfection from you. You are a spiritual being who is here to learn lessons and go on a journey of this life. Make sure you learn the lesson and release yourself from the pain and into a world of freedom. Maya Angelou said it best: "You made the best decision based on the information you had at the time." Stop beating up on yourself.

I realized that the battle was within me. When I figured out it was my choice to be happy, it became easier to be in motion with living my life. After seeing the mistakes in other women, it helped me to identify what caused pain to my soul. My heart led me to underestimate others. My insecurities enabled me to look past the trickery that my ex-husband and ex-boyfriends dumped on my shoulders. Women must step out of a dreadful relationship to see how the situation was not truthful.

Live your life as if the world is ending tomorrow. Pay no attention to those who don't want to see you advance. They envy your strength and ability to set goals and to make your dreams come true. Today, I appreciate how vital it is to go after my dreams and live out my passion for entrepreneurship. Today, I can see myself as a refined woman who has experience and knowledge to offer an employer, a good man, and my clientele. I know that I am worthy of love. I know that I bring good ideas, unconditional love and an array of qualities to a marriage, a relationship, and friendships.

Whatever happens is for a reason; learn from it. Every potential decision follows with an action – good or bad. I lived through rough storms but managed to breathe again. GOD heard my calls for help. He was there as a witness to my ex-husband cheating on me.

Stay true to what you believe in. When you second-guess yourself – so will others. They will decrease your chances of success, love and happiness. Never compromise your religious beliefs to make others comfortable. When you ask, ask GOD directly and do not go through someone else. Pray for yourself and others, even those who detest and despise you. They need blessings from GOD, too.

This book is my baby. From the thought of writing it, to the first day a letter was written and typed. As an avid book reader, achieving this goal wasn't outside my reach. GOD decreed a plan for me and it unfolded. Your story doesn't end until you breathe your last breath. The plan began the day of conception in my mothers' womb. It happened not when I wanted it to, but exactly how it was supposed to happen for me.

Of course, as a human being, we will have regrets from time to time. Now through this book, I see that life is what you make it. If you take charge of your life, you'll be able to shape the outcome from your actions. When you see the positive to events that seem to have a dreary outcome, it creates a clearer picture for your future. Stay positive, even when you don't see or understand the outcome to a situation. Remember, they are life lessons to live through and learn from – no matter what others say or what they do to you.

The lesson that I've learned while going through the marital process is this: look outside of your front door. The man of your dreams may not look like you, sound like you or come from your neighborhood. Understand that every man you meet won't cheat on you or deceive you. Be open-minded and prepared for a challenge. Perhaps, it's time to re-think your strategy on what you're looking for and what you can offer this person once he's in your life.

When you're praying to GOD for a husband, be specific. Your priorities should be less about what you want and more about what you need to be a successful wife. It doesn't matter what type of car he drove or how expensive his shoes costs. Your Lord will send to you an intelligent man with respect, honor, integrity and good character. Pray that you're equally yoked. When you disagree, take it to your Lord. Go ole school, when he asks you to be his wife, he should get permission from your father or someone you look up to that's in your life. Your father will be honored that he called him to take the responsibilities of being his daughter's husband. It's a matter of respect.

> These words are from a song that Chaka Khan wrote and sung that I can't get out of my head: "When your heart is free, it is easy to make a decision. When your head is clear, you know you have good judgments. Then your life is turning topsy-turvy and you have no reasons for what is disturbing you. Remember the words my father said to me. He said, keep your head up don't say you love him.

Walk away from all that is hurting you. Find your power you know you're strong, make that step and it will help you move on. When your mind is at peace, sleep comes so peacefully. When you start to dream, they are wonderful and sweet. Why give up? This time you can win. Why give up? This battle is within. Why stay when you know what he is going to do? Why choose him when it is time to choose YOU?"

GOD created me to live on this Earth to go through the fire of destruction, enormous trials, tribulations, sadness and happiness. This is my life. The smoke is gone. Breathing is better now for me because I turn to GOD when choking and panting for air. There are no doubts in my mind that in time everything that GOD has in store for me will come to pass, and 'now' I'm ready for the challenge!

Acknowledgements

First, I want to thank Allah for guiding and blessing me through my trials, tribulations and life lessons.

Daddy – You're the man who set the stage for my future. I wished that I could've grown up in the house with you as I became a wife and a Mother. You're the serious and outspoken parent who doesn't hesitate to speak your mind. I love and respect you unconditionally!

To My Closest Girlfriends: (who are my sisters in my heart)

Myrtle Elaine Hofler (Fatimah Ali) – My elementary school typing teacher and my sister in Islam. Thank you for teaching me how to reach my goals, for supporting me in Islam, and for being my spiritual and religious companion, as well as a Mother/sister figure. I love you forever!

Keshia Dail – We have sat up countless nights exchanging thoughts and offering each other advice through our trials and tribulations of life. We've been close friends/BFFs since high school. The bond we share is unusual to most; only a few can understand it. You're my sister from another Mother. I love you!

Bridget Turner – You've provided a safe haven for me through my transition back to Jersey in 2005 and a friendship full of love and support since the 5th grade. Unconditional sisterhood is what we share. Seeing your face during my mom's passing, brought a smile to my heart! Your motivation to succeed inspires me. I love you! You rock!

Lise Richards – Thank you for helping me cultivate my entrepreneurial spirit, and for continuously being excited and supportive of my passion for developing my business. Although living in different states has divided our friendship, you will always be my trusted friend. Your business savvy is infectious and you inspire me. I love you!

Wanda McKiver – Thank you for giving me the inspiration to move forward with my book. When I attended your book-signing party, it empowered my spirit. Your excitement is contagious!

Michele (Letoya) Taylor-Scott – Thank you for volunteering to provide your extensive English skills to my masterpiece at the beginning of this process. Your creative critique set the tone and format of what was missing. Your dedication in this venture will never be forgotten! I love you!

Tanya Brown – I don't know how to express my feelings for you. When we're on the phone or in person, we laugh so hard that it hurts my head! You're a breath of fresh air! I love you forever! As Kenny Bobien sang, "You are my friend."

Kimberly Moye – It seems like we've been friends forever! Living in North Carolina without family; you became my BFF in a short period of time. We started a new job that ignited our friendship. We clicked! I tell you all the time: I surround myself with smart and intelligent people. Your body weight challenges are inspirational. Your motivation and dedication to being healthy keeps me on my toes. I've learned a lot about you and your husband. I thank you from the bottom of my heart for helping me with editing of my book. What would I have done without you! You're family without the bloodline! I love you like a sister!

Ameenah Muhammad-Diggins – As my book coach, thank you for coming into my life to help me publish my book. It took all of these years for me to ask for help. Finally, after watching you online, I realized that we had the same entrepreneurial spirit. You gave me the insight, tools and resources to self-publish within a few months. Allah is merciful and you're a blessing to me.

Jason Graves – You came highly recommended. To be able to have a direct contact list of professionals adds immediate success to my entrepreneur journey. I plan to use your services for my next book and other editorial projects in the near future for my business. Thank you!

These individuals have been in my corner without questions or doubts. It's my belief that my friends are a replication of me. My friendships were never affected by our personal, business or religious viewpoints.

Last, but certainly not least – To the overwhelming number of people who played an instrumental part of my life, I wish I could individually name all of you. Please know that you're a part of my thoughts, my past and future. Continue being you!

Made in the USA
Columbia, SC
16 March 2020